My Dau

was an Astronaut

Stories & Poems

by **Write Now!**

the Suffolk Writers' Group

wnp

write now! publications

First Published in 2011
by Write Now! Publications
14 Hambrook Close,
Gt Whelnetham,
Bury St Edmunds,
Suffolk IP30 0UX

Printed by Abbeyhine Ltd, Bury St Edmunds, Suffolk

For permission to reprint or broadcast these stories
or poems write to Write Now! Publications.

ISBN-13: 978-0-9570202-0-7

Typeset by Inverse
Cover by WKJ Designs

ACKNOWLEDGEMENTS

Acknowledgements are due to all the writers who submitted their work for this collection.

Thanks also to Oliver Kemp for his help with the cover design.

The picture of the smiling girl on the cover is used with permission under the Creative Commons license Attribution-ShareAlike 3.0 Unported (CC BY-SA 3.0).

We are also indebted to David Pescod for his help in shaping this book.

Foreword

'There is nothing to writing. All you do is sit down at a typewriter and open a vein.'

It is many years since the famous American sports writer, Walter "Red" Smith, penned those words and, though today typewriters have given way to word-processors, the physical and emotional outpouring which a writer must undergo in the creative process has not changed. This collection of poetry and prose represents the 'blood' of members of the Bury St Edmunds writers' group, 'Write Now!' It is an eclectic mix of humour, romance, philosophy, black comedy—a volume you can dip into for a chuckle or a tear with your morning coffee, bedtime nightcap, or any moment in between.

David Richmond

CONTENTS

Won't Do You No Harm

Barry Baddock

I'd been waiting at Oakley for an hour when the soiled blue Lincoln drew up. The driver cleared a space in the back seat so I could add my pack to his suitcase, his military-green sleeping bag and—yes!—his dolls. It was Captain Blood who first caught my attention. The round little fellow had a green pirate headdress and a bulbous eye that gave him a pitiful air and robbed him of his buccaneer fearsomeness. Propped in his corner, he stared at me in pouting distrust.

As we pulled away, I struck up conversation, to show I was a sociable type.

The driver—John was his name—was friendly enough too, but reticent. As is the manner of prairie folk, he preferred to reply with a smile where words could be avoided without discourtesy.

I asked him about Captain Blood. John laughed at the name I had chosen. Yeah, he'd made Captain Blood himself. Made them all. Out of modelling clay.

'It's kind of a hobby,' he said.

'Would you mind if I looked at the others?'

'Be my guest.'

So, twisting in my seat, I made acquaintance with them all. There was Belinda Bluetooth, flat on her back on the sleeping bag. Apart from the rabbit-like teeth, Belinda had straggly hair and pale, hypnotic eyes. Then there was the Witch, a bucolic dwarf with an exaggerated hook nose, and huge mad eyes which covered half of her face. Porky, a flat-faced little man, had thin slit green eyes and scarlet cheeks. The Drooler was a masterpiece. One of his eyes was grotesquely hidden in a bulge of black clay like an evil lizard's. From the Drooler's cavernous mouth, lifelike saliva oozed into the black crevices of his chin.

John had moulded all of these. He had gotten hold of rags in bold gypsy colours: vermilions and purples and intense shades of green. He had kneaded and pried every face and every mouth into eerie silent expression. And he had painted the pupils of all the eyes. John had a talent for eyes. I told him so.

'Yeah,' he laughed, 'Yeah, maybe so.'

'I think old Belinda Bluetooth has the weirdest eyes,' I said. John smiled. 'Yeah, maybe. But she won't do you no harm.'

We entered Trego County as the August day was reaching its hottest. Thinking of the green sleeping bag behind me and of the war that was then flaring in South-East Asia, I asked if John had served in the military.

Yeah, he'd been in the army. Had I been in the army?

'No,' I said, 'I'm from Britain. And the British army didn't invite me.'

He smiled, in a charming, apologetic way. 'Aw, I guessed you weren't from these parts.'

A pensive silence. Then John went on to say that him joining the army—well, that was one big mistake. The army was tough, he found. Kinda tough all round. 'Specially tough in 'Nam. Na, he weren't in 'Nam for a whole lotta time. 'S matter of fact, in 'Nam, he'd discovered the yellow streak that'd been hiding in his backbone. So—a long, grim smile here—he was back. Oh, he'd had some psy-chee-atric therap-ee in Topeka. For a while. Coulda stayed longer. But he reckoned he'd just as soon be back home. In Ellsworth, Kansas. That's where he kept his modelling clay. And that's where he spent most-all his time. In his mobile home, working with the clay.

I listened in respectful silence to each slow-spaced sentence. The confessional character of John's monologue embarrassed me, and I was aware of having provoked it with my questions. So I decided to shut up for a while and tried to imagine him alone in his tiny home, pummelling, moulding and painting his beautiful clay monstrosities.

But soon, I became oppressed by the silence that had fallen between us and wondered if I had caused the man to brood. So, breaking the ice again, I asked where he was coming from.

From 'Frisco, he said calmly. John had a brother in 'Frisco. Well, not exactly 'Frisco. Chuck lived in one of them townships nearby, way up in California.

Did John like it there?

He thought about this one.

'Yeah?'—a questioning intonation—'First time I ever seen California.' Then, with a shy smile: 'I'm from these parts.' He waved a hand out at the prairies. 'Hot and flat and dry.' And we laughed.

Then, trundling eastwards through the long afternoon, John unfolded his story.

Not long after his discharge from the VA hospital in Topeka, John had heard from his brother. He didn't know how Chuck got to know about his—John's—circumstances. But there it was: a card, postmarked 'Frisco, waiting in the mailbox at the mobile home one night. Oh, John kinda knew that Chuck was up in that neck of the woods. But the brothers hadn't met or corresponded for—oh, coulda been eight, ten years.

Just short of WaKeeney, John suddenly pulled into a tiny rest stop and parked.

'I'll show yuh.'

Rummaging in the backseat junk, he found a tiny envelope

and gave it to me. The handwriting was mangled, infantile. It was a tribute to the postal services at both ends that the thing had ever been delivered.

Hi, John: (it said)
HoPe yoU have a happy Hoilday's
A hug for Susi From Me
Im Fine + daNdy.
MiSS You   Chuck

Who was Susi? Aw, Sue. That was John's ex-wife. Naw, it didn't amount to much, that marriage. They was just a coupla starry-eyed kids. They'd known each other since fifth grade and got married right after John was drafted. High school sweethearts, kinda. But it was, like, one big mistake. Sue and him. In the end, they just shook hands, and parted best of friends. Like, maybe three, four months later. No hard feelings. Seemed like Chuck didn't get to hear about the divorce. John had no idea where Sue was now. She married again, right soon after, to a lawyer guy. But she weren't in Ellsworth no more.

Without the breeze of the open road, the heat of the rest stop was crushing. Every half-minute, a truck thundered by. In the fields around us screamed a million invisible crickets.

Then John handed over Chuck's photograph, and sat gazing at me expectantly. It was a flash picture, shot in a living room. Smiling shyly into the camera, his pudgy arms spread across a sofa, was Chuck. His appearance, like his name, suggested a friendly, good-ole-boy type. He was a short, forgettable fellow with thinning hair and a white T-shirt.

Lolling beside him on the sofa were five or six rag dolls, with straw hair and painted faces. The girls wore farming smocks, the boys hillbilly overalls and straw hats. Each round face bore small painted eyes, a simple grin and two dabs of red, to signify healthy cheeks.

'So,'—I handed back the picture—'that's Chuck.'

I really could not find anything more intelligent to say.

John, without a word, restarted the car and drove on, staring ahead.

As we passed WaKeeney and Big Creek, I strove to think ahead of the story, and to fill in the gaps between those sparse, laconic utterances of John's.

I glanced sideways at him.

'So, you've been to see Chuck.'

He nodded, staring ahead at the road.

'But you didn't see him.'

A pause. Then: 'Nope.'

I closed my eyes and tried to imagine what might have happened after John had driven two thousand miles to reach his brother's home.

We passed Russell. The road's surface radiated the heat of the day, like a shimmering mirage. Behind us, in garish array, sprawled John's clay artifacts, Captain Blood gazing balefully at the back of John's head.

I spoke up again.

'You could have seen him, like you wanted to. It would have been a lovely surprise for him, seeing you.'

I paused for John's reply. But, staring ahead, he said nothing.

'You could have given him the dolls, like you wanted to. It would have been the major event of his year.'

Even as I heard myself saying this, I knew it was bullshit. I thought of John in Vietnam, John in the psychiatric ward. Of John's sad little divorce and weird artworks of clay. I thought of him in his mobile home, damaged, alone, slipping inch by inch into the morass, and grasping at his fragile edifice of illusions.

And I saw Chuck, shy-smiling, brotherly Chuck, with his half-literate words of comfort—a hug for Susi, happy hoildays, miss you—and Chuck's quiet suburban home, with a grass forecourt, maybe, and an ankle-high fence. And inside, Chuck's own tiny family of rag dolls.

And I imagined John gazing at Chuck's place for a long time. Then realising how suspicious it looked, a man in a dirty car, parked in a respectable neighbourhood, staring at a house that didn't belong to him. And I pictured him, with that fear of the law common to those living on the edge, furtively slipping into gear and pulling away.

And I knew why John had returned from California, bringing all of his creatures back with him

At Dorrance exit, we pulled off Interstate 70 and halted.

'This do you?'

'Oh, yes. I can get a ride from here. Probably make Salina by nightfall.'

'Sure hope you do.' He raised his eyebrows in encouragement.

I hauled out my pack. At the same time, John, twisting round, dragged together all the dolls and got them in a heap on his lap. Grooming and smoothing them with a graceful hand, he asked me:

'You like one o' these?'

'That's very kind of you,'—I was keen to avoid saying anything which might touch a chord of sadness in the man —'are you sure you can spare one?'

'Oh, yeah.' Then, with that small, apologetic smile, he added, 'I guess it was all one big mistake.'

I took Belinda Bluetooth. John placed the others in a heap beside him. We shook hands through the open window.

'It was very nice meeting you,' I said.

'Sure was a pleasure talkin' to you.' And, with a U-turn which raised a cloud of red dust, he was off and covering the last miles to Ellsworth.

I didn't have to wait long. An eastbound trucker picked me up as a wonderful orange sun slid towards the horizon.

The driver ground through the gears and soon we were full steam ahead on the Interstate. The engine's blare drowned all normal talk, so I just sat with my arms around my pack. Belinda Bluetooth was perched on top, her still, hypnotic eye fixed on the driver.

As we eased off in Salina, he glanced at her and grinned.

'Ma-an, you got a weird one there.'

I turned Belinda to me and studied the painted face and straggly hair.

'Maybe,' I replied. 'But she won't do you no harm.'

THE STAIRS

Carolyn Belcher

When I was sitting on the stairs,
I met a man who wasn't there.
He wasn't there again today.
I wish that man would go away.

'Jake, Jake.' His mother's voice sounded tired. 'I'm just popping out to the shops. Will you…? What are you doing there, love?'

'Nothing.' He didn't want her to ask any more questions. 'I'm playing a game.'

She walked up the few steps to where he was sitting, and sat down beside him.

'What game?' she asked.

'The man who wasn't there, game.'

She ruffled his hair. 'You're a funny boy,' she said. 'Jess's in her room, if you need anything. I shan't be long.'

'You said, "Will you…?" Will you what?'

'I don't know. Will you be all right, I expect. Will you?'

No. I'm never all right, not since…'Can I come with you?'

'But you hate shopping,' said his mother.

'I don't mind if it's not supermarket shopping.'

'Rock-a-bye baby

9

On the treetop.
When the wind blows
The cradle will rock.
When the…

Jake jumped up, almost knocking his mother off the step.
'Did you hear that, Mum?'

'Careful, love,' she said. 'Hear what?'

'Nothing.' He knew what would happen if he told her. She
would make an appointment for him to see Dr. Rees. And Dr.
Rees would ask him more questions. He might even suggest
hypnosis. He'd mentioned hypnosis once or twice in past
sessions.

'If we don't get to the bottom of this, Jake, we can always
try hypnosis.'

He said things that Jake was thinking, like, 'You feel safe on
the stairs, don't you, Jake?'

He did, and that was why he couldn't go up; he couldn't go
down, not while his mother was out. He wasn't able to block
out the voice, the song, but the man couldn't get him.

His mother looked at him for what seemed like a long time,
then she shrugged. Andrew recognised she wasn't going to
try to persuade him to come down. He knew what shopping
was needed; she couldn't get to sleep without her pills, and
she didn't have any left. Andrew knew this because he had
taken the strip out of the box the day before, and flushed the
remaining few down the lavatory, replacing the strip in the
box afterwards. It had taken several attempts to get rid of
them, and he'd been forced to fetch the rolling pin from the
drawer in the kitchen, and crush the pills to powder in the
bottom of the pan. Afterwards, he'd washed the rolling pin;
not that anyone used it; his mum bought frozen puff pastry
if she made a pie, which was not very often now. His father
used to like pies, especially blackcurrant ones. The currants

reminded Andrew of rabbit droppings.

Bye baby bunting, Daddy's…

At breakfast that morning, Andrew could see how tired his mother looked. Jilly didn't come down for breakfast at weekends; she stayed in bed, sometimes until lunchtime. He was aware his mother had had a disturbed night. She'd heard his screams when the nightmare came, and had rushed into his bedroom, held him, stroked his damp forehead, wiped his tears, chased the ghost away, and last of all, changed his bedding, telling him it didn't matter: lots of children wet their beds for all sorts of reasons.

Andrew felt that the words were to comfort, not the truth. He knew he was not normal; other children his age didn't wet the bed, other children didn't see ghosts who wanted to harm them, and…he didn't want to think about the ghost again, invite him back, that and bed-wetting was why their doctor had made an appointment for him to see Dr. Rees in the first place.

He felt sick—the ghost would be back, invited or not, and Andrew was aware he couldn't continue to flush his mother's pills down the lavatory; she would become suspicious, would realise something was happening to them. He would have to sit half way up the stairs if she went out during the day, and try to get there, at night, if the ghost came into his room. He didn't always come. But Andrew went to bed afraid, and tried hard not to fall asleep. The ghost was always angry; he would scream the rhyme louder, and louder but he would not go down the stairs, not again.

Andrew refused to give the ghost the name, Daddy, Dad, Father. No father ought to have behaved as he had done. Besides, the ghost didn't look like his father. He howled out the song, but his face was expressionless.

Alive, his father had had lots of different faces, a happy face, a sad face, a jokey face, and a serious face. Then there was the face that turned grotesque with anger because Andrew had wet himself; he didn't seem to be able to help it, what with the rough games and the tickling.

'You little shit,' his father would yell. And Andrew would cower on the floor, where he had been dropped, waiting for the blows and kicks he knew would come.

Later there was the tearful face, and when his mother got back, the lying face.

'We were having a game of chase before bed-time,' he would say. Silly lad fell down the stairs; tripped up; slipped; the excuses for the bruises were endless. 'I thought I was going to have to take him to hospital.'

And his mother believed him. After all, why should she not? He had never lifted a finger against her, nor against either of his children, in her presence. Andrew said nothing. He didn't know what to say.

One day, he decided he'd had enough. He dreaded his mother going out because of the pain he knew he would have to endure. He had to make it stop.

Rough and tumble games always happened upstairs in his bedroom, and there was a pattern to the evenings. After tea, he, his sister and father watched the television, always a little later than was normally allowed. His father had a six-pack of lager, and they had cokes. The evening of the plan, Andrew had Mr. Duster, his monkey comforter, beside him, inside which were some marbles. Mr. Duster used to be a hot water bottle cover, but Andrew didn't have a hot water bottle any longer; hot water bottles were sissy. When bedtime came, they all went upstairs, Jilly to her room and music-while-you-text; Andrew to...'Dad,' he said, 'I've forgotten Mr. Duster.'

'You're too big a boy for that old monkey,' said his father.

'He likes to watch our games,' said Andrew, holding his breath.

'Oh very well, go and get him,' said his father. 'But I'm going to have to speak to your mother about it. I think Mr. Duster ought to be thrown away now, he's no longer of any use.'

If Andrew had experienced any doubts about what he intended to do, those words fixed his resolve. He went downstairs, picked up Mr. Duster, and on the way back he placed marbles on each step. He knew he would have to be careful to avoid them, and would have liked to have a practice run but he couldn't do that; his father would be suspicious about the length of time he was taking. He left one side free from danger and repeated to himself as he went back to his bedroom; 'Go down safe side; run away down the safe side.'

As I was going down the stairs,
I met a man who wasn't there.
He wasn't there again today.
I wish that man would go away.

THE SWAN

Laura Haines

The Swan

(Inspired by walking along the river Itchen in Winchester at night).

Constellations prick through
The film of the water's surface.
Gathering the mist
Upon its phantom wings
A white swan
Catches the moon's porcelain glance
And scatters the stars
Unafraid.

THE FLINT WALL

Rose O'Meara

The paper fell onto the mat with a thump. Must be Friday then, she thought, as she poured boiling water into the teapot for the first cup of the day; Bury Free Press day. The paper could wait until she'd had her tea. She arranged the tea things neatly on the tray and carried it through to her sitting room. There was little enough to fill her long and lonely days, but she did like looking through the paper at all the Golden Wedding photographs to see if she recognised anyone.

Sitting in her armchair sipping tea, she thought about all those couples, wondering what sort of life they had led together and what must it be like to have lived with one person for so many years. She could have married if she'd wanted to, of course she could. After the war there was that boy from the corn merchants, always hanging around after he'd delivered the feed, what was his name…urm…Arthur, … Arthur Newnham, that was it. He was very eager; she could have married him if she'd wanted to. Her Dad had been very keen, feeling the need to get her married off as soon as possible after what had happened, not to mention getting his feedstuffs at a discount. Shop-soiled he had called her. If he's willing to have you, you take him, that's what he had said, you won't get anyone else. But she wouldn't. She wasn't going to have just anybody, not after…no.

Raining again and it looked as if it had set in for the day—the sky was grey and gloomy. If it was dry this afternoon, maybe she could pop into town and go to the Library. It was always nice and warm in there, and sometimes you could have a little chat with one of the assistants if they weren't too busy. Busy, keep busy, that was it, that's the way to go, none of this sitting around remembering. But there wasn't much to keep her busy in the tiny flat, she didn't even have a window box. Mum had loved her flowers. Dahlias, they were her favourite, great big splashes of colour every summer, all down the front path and along the flint wall each side of the front gate. Bright reds, yellows, scarlet and pink.

As she sat, alone and quiet in her sitting room, she remembered that rough and knobbly wall in front of the farm house. It was full of round orange and brown flints, shiny and jet black where they had been knapped, the knife-sharp edges ready to slice through even hard and calloused hands. Like his. She shut her eyes for a moment and rested her head against the chair back. Instead of rain splattering against the windows, she could hear the sound of his trowel as he worked the mortar between the flints and feel the warmth of that long-ago summer sun.

When she picked up her cup, the tea was stone-cold and she realised she must have been day-dreaming again. She took the tea tray out to the kitchen, collected the paper from the mat, and sat down at the little table. She thought she might just have a quick look at the Deaths and the Golden Weddings while she ate her breakfast. She scanned quickly through the paper to find the photos, but there were no faces she knew this week and no names she recognised in the Deaths column either. She sighed. She quite liked to find that she had outlived her contemporaries. She took the paper back to the sitting room and started her daily routine of tidying and cleaning. The only personal touch in the sparsely furnished room was a sepia photograph of her mother in an ornate silver frame. Every day she picked up the photograph, dusted it carefully and replaced it, exactly in the centre of the mantelpiece. Her mother was pictured sitting in a deck chair outside the farm house, with a bunch of flowers on her lap, one hand across her forehead shielding her eyes from the brightness of that long-ago summer sun.

As she pushed her lightweight vacuum cleaner around, she remembered keeping house for her Father. Mangles, scrubbing brushes, stiff brooms and washing soda had been the order of the day. How hard it had been. He'd only lived for another five years after Mum went, and, as it was a tied house, she'd had to find somewhere else to live. They gave her a couple of months grace, but a new tenant farmer needed the house and so she had to go. It was June 1953.

It was June when they'd met, and a Monday. Monday the 27th of June, 1944. She was seventeen. It had been a hot dry month after a long spell of rain, and the old lime mortar in the front flint wall had crumbled and the wall collapsed. Her Dad didn't have the skill or the time to make repairs, and so the Land Agent had arranged for someone to come up from the POW camp down the road. Her Dad wouldn't have any truck with him at all, not even when he saw how hard he worked, wouldn't have had him at all if he'd had his way. Bloody Kraut he used to say, keep him out of my way. Her Mum had been a bit softer and made sure that he had water to drink and bread and cheese to eat, but she wouldn't take it out to him, that had been her job.

Feeling suddenly tired, she put away the vacuum cleaner and her cleaning things, sat down and closed her eyes. A few minutes rest was what she needed. Today was going to be one of those days, a head full of memories and aching joints, and wretched rain.

One of the first things she'd noticed about him were his

teeth, strong and white, as he tore hungrily into the food she brought him, not stopping until every morsel was gone and the enamel plate clean. Then he drained the water, handed mug and plate back to her and smiled. Oh, he was so handsome! It wasn't long before he was all she could think about. Every morning she watched and waited impatiently for the camp transport which dropped him off at the gate and then took him away in the evenings, leaving her longing for his return.

As the days passed, she felt his eyes follow her whenever she went outside to feed the hens or peg out the washing, so she found more and more reasons to be there. She worked on the vegetable plot, weeded the flower borders and fetched more cold water from the well for him on hot days. At lunchtime they took to sitting down together on the road side of the flint wall while she waited for him to finish his food. Sitting there, they couldn't be seen from either the house or the fields beyond. He told her about his life in Germany before the war, about his mother and his little sister. Neither of them spoke about the war. From their first tentative hand hold to a quick snatched kiss to making love in the hay barn opposite seemed very natural and right. They were young and passionate and desperate to be together.

Lying in the barn together after making love, enclosed and isolated by the sweet-smelling hay, they had made wonderful plans for the future. They thought their love would last forever; it was so strong and certain. After the war was over he would come back for her and they would go to America together, far away from Europe and the chaos of war. They would make a new life for themselves and bring up their children in peace and love. *Ich liebe dich*, I love you, he had said, *ich liebe dich*.

As the long intense summer days of love and secrecy passed, she began to fret about what would happen when the flint wall was finished, but the ending was more sudden and brutal than she could have imagined. One morning the transport had turned up much later than usual. She had been waiting in the garden for him and saw at once that something was different. Without worrying who could see them he had taken both her hands in his. He told her that he was to be repatriated to Germany the next day and had been allowed out of camp only to collect his tools. In his hand he held a gold ring, his mother's wedding ring which she had given him when he joined the Africa Corps. He had put the warm ring in her hand, closed her fingers tightly around it and told her he would be back. *Ich liebe dich*, I love you, *ich liebe dich*. I will be back, I promise I will be back, I promise, and then he was gone.

But he never did come back, and when she came home alone after having the baby, she wrapped the ring in a piece of oilcloth and poked it into a crevice in the flint wall.

After she had finished reliving the story of her lost love, she sat quietly in her chair, eyes closed, hands clasped in her lap for a long time, and when she opened her eyes the rain had stopped and a yellow autumn sun was lightening the room. She looked around her. It was difficult, sometimes, to come back to the present. She thought she might stay at home for the rest of the day, not bother with going out. The paper was beside her and so she picked it up again and started reading. The article was on page five. Keith Wilkes, 43, local builder, had found a gold wedding ring hidden in a flint wall he was repairing and had traced the owner through the inscription. It had belonged to a German woman who had given it to her son when he went off to fight in the Second World War. Mr. Wilkes said he had been intrigued by the ring and had spent a long time tracing its history. He had been over to Germany and had personally given the ring back to Emil Schmitt, the woman's son. And there, right in front of her, was a picture of Emil surrounded by his wife, his children and his grandchildren, taken on the occasion of their Golden Wedding.

Overwhelmed by grief and anger, she laid the paper slowly down on her lap. No, she wouldn't go out this afternoon.

Delfina

George Wicker

I am hiding in Don Rico's old house, and through the window I see a black Mercedes pull up. A man gets out of the driver's side wearing dark sunglasses. He is bald, and has a silver earring in one ear. He opens the passenger door, and a fine looking woman emerges. She wears a blue trouser suit, the jacket finished with cream piping around sleeves and collar. There is a hat, just wide enough to keep the sun off her shoulders. Suddenly she turns and I duck beneath the window. When I return to my position she is entering the house across the road. The driver has disappeared, but then I see him at the back of the car. His shirt has short sleeves, and he puffs his cheeks as he lifts a large suitcase from the boot down onto the cobbles. Then I know it is true—Delfina has come home.

Only a week before, Raphael told me it would be so, but I didn't believe him. I even bet chores with him, taking on the cleaning of the big barn for a fortnight on the truth of his tale. 'The Señorita will be back,' he said, 'and you will regret it.'

'Never,' I told him, 'not a chance. The river will engulf Acara before we see her return.'

He nodded slowly. My brother is a patient man, and I should have known he would not bet on lies. And now that the evidence is before me, the lost bet seems unimportant. Even my curse, on the town that lies in the valley below our village, is insignificant in the fact of her return.

I continue my vigil at the window, and after an hour I see the driver emerge from the house into the hot afternoon sun. He looks up at the sky, dabs his forehead with a handkerchief, then gets into the car, reverses it down the road, and swings around in a gateway. He drives past the other farms and hillside cottages, down the valley road toward Acara. I watch the car and the dust thrown up by its wheels until it is lost in the distance. Then I turn my attention back to the house. Somewhere, in that whitewashed and dark-windowed building, she remains.

Raphael is exuberant when I see him later. I find him at the farm, where he is feeding chickens at the back of the barn. 'Ha, so I was right after all,' he says, and gathers his waistcoat off a stool, adding, 'this is your job now.'

He goes into the house and comes out with a bag. Ten minutes later we are both crouched under Don Rico's window, our bikes hidden out of sight behind the back door. Breathless, we sit there panting, until I kneel up and peer through the cracked and dirty glass.

'What's happening?' he asks.

'Nothing,' I say.

He moves to the other side of the window and shields his eyes against the light. 'Is she alone?'

'Yes.'

'Then how did she get here?'

I tell him about the dark Mercedes, the bald driver and the suitcase. He starts humming. 'She is here for a while then,' he murmurs.

After a few minutes we slide down to the floor. Raphael reaches into the bag and pulls out a loaf, which he shares with me. We take turns to gulp homemade apple juice from the bottle that we pass between us under the window. Across the stone floor of Don Rico's kitchen dust swirls in the beams of sunlight coming through the window. The heat is stifling. While most of the townspeople of Acara are having their siesta, our mother will still be working at the laundry in the village, while Papa will be resting at the side of the big field of sunflowers and olives which constitutes most of our farm, until it is cool enough to continue outside.

'We must be vigilant,' Raphael says when I suggest we do the same.

'Tell me about her then,' I say, 'to keep me awake.'

'All right.' He swigs from the bottle, tears a piece of bread from the loaf and holds it in his right hand. 'Once, this was Delfina,' he says, and thrusts the hand forward. 'She was plump, unattractive, just someone from the village that no-one looked twice at. Then something happened.'

'What?'

Raphael is in no hurry with his tale, and he chews on the bread as he speaks. 'Well, she worked at the bakery in Acara where her father was foreman, making loaves, breads and pastries. She also made fancy cakes for weddings, celebration days, that sort of thing.'

'Yes, yes, I know all that—tell me what happened.'

'She was dusty, always covered in flour. Fat from eating too much dough. Yet there was something wild about her, and boys said she would be easy with them. Sometimes.'

Raphael is seventeen, I am three years younger, and there are things he talks about that I do not fully understand.

'Easy?'

'Yes, easy. Free with her affections.'

'Oh,' I cannot equate the fine woman I saw that morning with the lump of bread in my brother's hand. 'Is that all?'

'No, it is not.' Raphael takes another bite of bread, another swig from the bottle. 'There was a big party planned, at a rich man's villa a few miles down the river. The bakery was given the commission to supply all the cakes, meringues and sweets for the party. It was a large order for a small bakery, but the baker was doing well out of it, and he got all the staff, including Delfina, to work extra hours so that the order would be met.'

I listen as he tells how Delfina met a man at the party, and eight months later, heavily pregnant, moved with him to the city. I remember that a big car turned up that day too. Mama refused to let me watch with the others, instead putting me to clean the stable, where the horses snorted and stamped as I swept around them.

'There was a terrible commotion,' Raphael continued. 'She was crying, the baker was crying, but they waved her off, in the big car. Some of the townspeople mocked and shouted.'

'Why?'

'Because of her reputation. People think about such things.'

It is hot, and outside a loose shutter on the side of the house slaps a regular beat against the wall. I can hear swifts squealing as they gather insects high above in the cloudless sky. In my mind I picture Delfina, there in her father's house, opening shutters and windows that have been closed since his death, letting flies and light into silent rooms. I imagine she would have removed her hat by now, and jacket perhaps, laying them carefully on a table, letting her long black hair drop down onto shoulders covered by a white and carefully pressed blouse...'

'Julio! Wake up. Have you listened to any of my story?'

I tell him my daydream.

'Don't worry about her,' he says, then laughs. 'She is too hot for you.' He hands me the bottle, tosses what is left of the bread in my lap and stands up. 'Don't sit here for ever—remember, you have chores to do.'

I hear him scrabbling on his bike across the gravel outside. *Too hot for you*—what does he mean?

When I return home later, Mama asks me where I've been.

'Nowhere,' I say, as I start on the olives, salad leaves and soft cheese she places before me.

'Really, because I heard you were in Don Rico's old place again.'

'No!' I feign indignation.

'Raphael told me.'

'Oh.'

'He also tells me you have bartered some chores with him, and lost. Will you ever learn?'

'Sorry, Mama.'

'Good. You see, I know everything.' She smiles, wiping hands on her apron as she returns to the sink. 'Now, tell me why you were there,' she says over her shoulder.

'Well,' I begin, my mouth full of olives. Did she really know the truth about Delfina?

'I was resting there, after the ride up from the town. It was midday, and I was sheltering from the sun. Then I heard a noise, a car coming up the road.'

'Yes, I know about the car. And your siestas in the cottage too. Except that this time—and don't lie, because I know everything—it wasn't about sleep was it? Or avoiding your chores?'

'No, Mama,' I say honestly. 'Raphael told me that señorita Delfina was coming home. I thought I would see it for myself, you know, as I missed her departure.' I make a mental note to repay my brother for his treachery.

'It doesn't matter why, I do not want you near that house again.'

'But...'

'It is wrong. That woman has returned to tie up her dead father's affairs. She will be gone again in a few days. That is an end to it.'

'Did you know her, Mama?'

'Yes, and even in the days when her hair was crusted with flour and her hands were singed from the ovens, she always believed she was better than the rest of us.'

'How do you mean?' and I think of Raphael's explanation that Delfina was like the bread itself, linked with the bakery, plump with generosity.

'You are too young, 'Lio, and your brother doesn't understand either. Will you promise me?'

'Of course, Mama.'

The next morning I am back at Don Rico's. I sit under the window again, and get cheese and a bottle from my bag. I am preparing to eat, when there is a knock at the door. My heart freezes—surely my mother has not followed me from the house?

'Hello?' It is a woman's voice. My chest pounds, and I press back into the wall.

'I know someone is in there,' she says.

The door opens slowly, and Delfina stands framed in the light that spills into the room through the doorway. She looks straight at me. I wonder if there is room to rush past her, as I get to my feet, one hand holding my bag tightly to me, the other clutching the neck of the bottle.

'Are you spying on me?' she asks.

'I am just eating,' I say. 'I came here to rest.'

She walks in, and I can see her properly. She is wearing a long, flowing blue skirt, and the white blouse I had imagined the day before. Her brown arms are bare, except for some silver bangles at the wrist. She looks around the room, then comes over to the window and stands beside me, so close I can smell her perfume. She stares across to her father's house.

'I used to come here years ago, when I was a little girl. And look out from this very window, waiting for my father to come home.'

'I was not looking.'

'Hush,' she says, then turns to lay a finger lightly on my

mouth. 'There is no need to deny it—I am an interesting person. What is your name?'

'Julio, Señorita...Señora, Julio Muñiz, from the farm across the fields.' I point to the door.

'Julio,' she repeats, 'and it is Señorita. Not married.' She laughs. 'Is that full?' She gestures toward the bottle. I hold it out to her, she takes it, puts it to her mouth and leans her head back as she drinks. I see a drop run down her chin and fall onto the blouse.

She catches my stare. 'Ah,' she sighs, then looks at the bag. 'Do you have food?'

'Only cheese,' I say.

'Then, Julio, you shall come and eat with me.'

I follow her out of the old house into the hot sun. We walk round the back, through the yellowed grass, and across the rough cobbles of the road to the baker's house. I think of running away again, yet the thought of Raphael's face when he hears of my cowardice stops me. I enter the living room behind her. The shutters are closed, but they are old, and sunlight falls in lines across the table by the window. She motions for me to sit down, and goes into the kitchen. I hear drawers and cupboards open and close, then she is back with a tray, from which she places two glasses on the table in front of me, and plates on which are arranged a salad of leaves and tomatoes. She pours oil from a bottle on the table over them and gives me a fork. 'There is cake after this,' she says, as I pour the apple juice from my bottle into the glasses. I go to say something but she holds up her hand.

'Eat.'

After the meal she asks. 'Tell me, Julio, are people talking about my return?'

I nod.

'Then tell me what they are saying.'

I raise my eyes to look at her, and see an oval, tanned face, and brown eyes. She has dark freckles on the tops of her cheeks, full lips and I notice (how could I not notice) that the white blouse is unbuttoned along her throat.

'Are they glad I am back?'

'They say you are trouble.'

'Trouble! Your mother among them I expect. I know her, Señora Muñiz. Does she still work at the laundry?' I nod. 'Because she is your mother, I will not say anything against her. But the women all remember me badly, because I made one mistake.'

'What mistake? 'I ask.

'You must know why I left, although you were just a boy when they came for me.'

'Why did you let them?'

'I was pregnant, unmarried, carrying a stranger's child. Not just a stranger, but the son of a rich man, barely older than me. There was nothing else to be done.'

'They said you left for the city. Why did you not come back?'

She doesn't reply, but takes up the plates and glasses and goes into the kitchen. I fear I have upset her. There are noises in the kitchen, and she returns with cake, which I eat in silence. Then she leads me outside and tells me to go.

Her eyes are shining, and she no longer looks at me.

'Are you all right?' I ask.

'Come back tomorrow, if your mother lets you. We can talk again.'

The next day I have to do my chores, and I cannot get away. The morning after I wake early, take my bike and cycle down the valley path to Delfina's house. I take care to avoid the ruts in the road where the wheels of the tractors have churned up mud which has now set as hard as concrete. She is not there. After an hour of watching I return to the farm, lie on my bed, and think about her. What if she has left already? Later

Raphael comes in, and teases me.

'How are you enjoying my chores,' he mocks. 'Is she worth it?' I ask him what he means, and he laughs. 'I saw Delfina in the town today,' he says. 'At the bank. She has sold the house. I think she is taking her father's money away.'

I am relieved she is still here, and resolve to see her the next day, Friday, when the banks are shut and the shops close early. For the first time in a long while it is overcast, and the wind is strong. I knock on the door, which opens slowly. 'Come in,' she says, then whispers, 'Did anyone see you?'

'No.'

'Good. We don't want any more trouble.'

Today she is wearing an apron, and I notice her blouse is buttoned up to the chin. She seems agitated. We have cake again, sitting at her table, a traditional sponge meringue. She tells me she hasn't cooked for so long. I ask her what it is like living in the city. 'It is interesting,' she says, but then offers nothing more. 'Why did you not come yesterday?' she asks.

'I was busy—I came as soon as I could. When I did you were out.'

'I cannot stay in and wait for you. I have business to attend to.'

'I know. My brother saw you in town. At the bank.'

She looks at me for a long time, and then says, softly, 'Poor Julio, can you keep a secret?'

'Of course,' I say

'I am moving.'

'From here?'

She looks at me, her head to one side. 'I moved from here a long time ago.' Then she leans toward me, and ruffles my hair. 'Silly boy, did you think I was staying for ever? 'And then she says, 'Do you love me? Is that it? Is that why you spy on me?'

I am angry: first that she has ruffled my hair like a baby, then that she asks me such questions. She realises and holds my hand. 'I am sorry, Julio, but you are just a boy. Capable of love, I know, but do not fall in love with me.' She looks at me, with sad eyes, and gently squeezes my fingers. 'I am not worth it.' She whispers.,'I had a child, a boy, pretty like you, his father was so handsome.' Her voice trails off. 'Then they took him from me.'

For an instant, I think she is talking about the rich man's son. Then I realise. 'Oh.' I say.

'Do you believe that anyone could do such a thing? I was allowed to wean him. I called him Emesto, after his father, although he was never baptised with that name. Then, one day, three months after his birth, they came and took him. I was forced to sign papers and agree to many things. In return they gave me some money and a place to live.' Her voice fails and her shoulders fall. Tears well in her eyes. 'I never saw my Emesto again.'

'Did you not fight them, tell your father? What about the rich man's son?'

'He was taken from me as well. Packed off to college, or the army. Oh yes, they looked after me, as they promised, found me a job as a nanny, with nice clothes and a good income, but everything I see in the children I look after reminds me of what I have lost.' She begins to sob. 'Oh, Julio, I hate it, hate every second of their grand lives. That is why, with the help of my father's money, I must get away.'

I can see how upset she is, but do not know what to do. I am confused. The Delfina I have imagined, who my mother scorns and my brother teases me about, is not the one crying before me.

We spend the afternoon together. The house is cool, her lips moist, and her skin soft. The loose shutter over on Don Rico's house bangs in the wind as we lie on the bed upstairs, and I discover the meaning of my brother's words. And when it is over I want to tell her that if she will stay until I am no longer a child, and not go back to the city, I will help her.

Then I think of my mother's words, and the promise made that I have already broken, and I cannot.

Two days later I am at the farm, cleaning out the stable, when Raphael rushes in.

'Julio, she is leaving. The big car has arrived; come quickly,' he gasps and dashes out, forgetting his bicycle and instead running wildly down the rutted path toward the village. I watch his flailing limbs until he is out of sight. Then I lift my broom and sweep the dust and hay from the corners of the stable into a heap in the middle, while the horses stamp and snort around me.

You

Eleanor Castleden

You decorate my bed
With your nakedness
You stimulate my senses
As I ride the waves of pleasure
You make me smile from within
Whilst you play incredible music
On my heart
Giving and receiving pleasure
Eyes wide open, staring deeply
Lovingly, remembering
My soul

LOOKING FOR MR SQUIRREL

Nigel George

Was this Dave Squirrel? The front of his suit stained with vomit and what looked like lumps of dried rogan josh? The file described him as a successful businessman with a drink problem and a love of curry, so the sleeping drunk fitted the bill. Still, Harry Trent wasn't sure. But then, Harry wasn't sure of very much. He'd arrived for his first day as a trainee with Clancy Burns Solicitors to be immediately given a file and thrust into a taxi. Alex Small, one of the partners, had jabbered at him about how important Squirrel was and off he'd been sent. Ten minutes ago, the cab had stopped outside the court and Harry bounded up the steps. So far he hadn't been able to find his client, or his client's barrister or even which court he was supposed to be in. The place was a sea of tattooed men, shaved heads and young girls with screaming infants. A clutch of people in sharp suits herded them back and forth like Gucci-clad sheepdogs.

So, was this sleeping drunk Dave Squirrel? Trent had asked every other candidate.

'Excuse me, Mr Squirrel?' Harry's "client" snored on. He leaned in closer, recoiling as the drunk's fetid breath sandpapered his face, 'Mr Squirrel?' Harry gently shook his shoulder and then, with a little more force, 'Mr Squirrel!'

'Wha? Who es callin' me a squirrel?'

Harry stepped back as the man looked at him through bloodshot eyes.

'Who are you?' he growled.

'My name is Harry Trent. I'm from your instructing solicitors.'

'Wha? You my solicitor?'

It didn't seem the time to argue the point, though Harry would later regret it. 'Yes,' he replied.

The drunk looked around, his large dirty hands searching for something. He pulled a tattered bag from his jacket and examined it minutely. Finally, he tore it to pieces before being convinced it was empty. He looked at Harry accusingly.

'Where es it?' he demanded.

Harry shook his head in bemusement. People around him were moving into court. Where was that bloody barrister? Was this Squirrel? He hadn't confirmed it.

'I'm sorry, what have you lost? Are you Mr Squirrel?'

The drunk staggered to his feet, flicking fragments of dried vomit at Harry as he brushed himself down.

'A am not Mr Badger! Or Mr Bunny Rabbit! And, A am not Mr Fucking Squirrel, neither! And if you don't give me back ma whiskey, a'm goin' to do you!'

Harry moved back—this kind of thing never happened on TV. Thankfully, an usher came across and put a hand on the drunk's arm.

'Come on, Jim,' he said soothingly. 'Let's get you into court.' The drunk looked into the calming eyes of the usher and allowed himself to be led away, muttering as he did so that it wasna fair for a grown man to be called a squirrel and they should get that bastard who'd stolen his whiskey.

Harry stood, slightly shaken, and then realised everyone had disappeared into the courtroom. He ran in after them and was guided to the second row of benches populated by solicitors and barristers. Harry hovered over his seat. Was it a good idea to have come in here? Shit, he didn't know…further thought was cut short.

'Silence in court.'

Everyone stood as the Stipendiary Magistrate emerged from behind a screen and took his seat at the head of the court. The first case was called—and Harry's funk began to grow. He had no idea where his client or the barrister were. He couldn't even be sure he was in the right court: the building housed ten of them.

'Call James Grange.'

Harry looked up and saw the old tramp he'd thought to be Squirrel walk into the dock. He was charged with one count of drunk and disorderly, and another of shoplifting.

'Mr Grange,' asked the Clerk. 'Are you represented today?'

'Oh, aye,' he replied with, a confident smile.

The Clerk waited expectantly for the lawyer representing Grange to rise. No one moved. He turned to Grange.

'Mr Grange, your solicitor doesn't seem to be in court. Who is it?'

'It's one of tha' lot', he said pointing at the benches of lawyers. The Clerk swung round to a sea of shaking heads. The Magistrate was getting agitated.

'Which one, Mr Grange?'

Grange looked hesitantly at the double bench of lawyers. He broke into a smile as he recognised Harry and pointed his grubby finger.

'Him!'

All eyes turned on Harry.

The Clerk shot Harry a stare. 'Mr…?' The look compelled him to stand.

'Trent…Harry Trent.'

'Do you represent this man?'

'No!'

'He does! He said he was ma solicitor!'

'No, I didn't!'

'HE DID! HE DID!'

The Magistrate joined in.

'Did you say you were this man's solicitor?'

'Well, yes, but…'

'But what? You either act for this man or you don't.'

'I don't, I'm not even a solicitor.'

'What! Why did you tell this man you were?'

'I didn't!'

'He shook me as well! And stole ma whiskey!' chimed in Grange.

'Is this true? Did you assault this man and steal his whiskey?' demanded the Magistrate.

Harry had often imagined his first day in the legal profession —it had never gone like this.

'Well?'

'No! I gave him a gentle shake, to wake him up. I've never seen his whiskey. I did tell him I was a solicitor, but that seemed the easiest thing to do at the time.'

'Let me get this straight: you impersonated a solicitor, assaulted this man, and stole his whiskey?'

'And he called me a squirrel,' added Grange indignantly.

'Why,' demanded the Magistrate, 'did you call this man a squirrel?'

'I called him Mr Squirrel', said Harry plaintively.

'Mr Trent,' said the Clerk, trying to restore order.

'It's a serious matter to pretend to be a solicitor when you're not. You also say you shook this man, and we have the matter of the missing whiskey—which should not have been brought into court in the first place,' he added, looking sternly at Grange. He turned back to Harry

'So, we have established you are not a solicitor.'

'No.'

'And you admit to assaulting this man?'

'No, I…'

'You shook this man?'

'Yes', said Harry resignedly.

'And what qualification, if any, do you hold?'

'I'm a trainee…solicitor.'

The Clerk turned to the Magistrate, who was starting to hyperventilate.

'Send him down,' he gasped. 'We'll deal with Mr Trent later.'

And so, two hours into his legal career, Harry was led to the cells.

On the Edge

David Richmond

A small, curved stage had been set up in the hotel's ballroom, and a pianist was seated at the grand piano, providing background music to the hum of conversation. I knew it was an "invitation only" event and among the two hundred or so guests who were seated at the tables, I recognised many of my colleagues. A couple of tables from where I sat with Louise, I saw Frank from the Telegraph, sitting with Gene Reynolds of Associated Press and Barton Fleming of Reuters. Gene was looking distinctly uncomfortable, I thought, with his ample paunch constrained by a purple cummerbund. His face was flushed and I suspected that he had already had rather too much to drink. Frank, as usual, had managed to achieve the casual smartness for which he was noted at such functions, his pale grey shirt, open at the neck, echoing the steel of his hair, and of a grey and white checkered scarf he wore. Barton appeared more interested in the extremely attractive brunette on his right than in whatever the other two were discussing. I presumed she was the latest in the long line of mistresses he had installed on his houseboat at Hammersmith.

I felt decidedly on edge. This was to be the biggest night of my career. I checked my shirt cuffs, discreetly showing slightly below the sleeve of my suit jacket, the gold cufflinks reflecting the light from the candle in the table's centre. Knowing that I would be on show, along with my work, I had dressed with particular care - a new suit from Bond Street, Russell & Hodge hand-made shirt, carefully-knotted silk tie, colourful without being flamboyant. I planned to look my best when my picture appeared in all the dailies the next day.

I became aware that the pianist had stopped playing and was leaving the stage. From either side, racks of spotlights gradually illuminated the microphone and lectern which stood at the front, while the rest of the lights in the room were dimmed. The conversation hushed and applause began as Russell Halliday, chairman of the Press Association, took to the stage.

'Ladies and gentlemen, friends and colleagues, it's my pleasure to welcome you this evening to this prestigious venue for this year's awards for outstanding press photography of the year. It's also a privilege to have been asked to chair the jury, all of whom were photographers who have made a unique contribution to our industry. Together we have had the difficult, but immensely enjoyable task of sifting through more than seven thousand photographs which represent the finest in our profession. I have to say that in my thirty five years as a staff photographer I have never seen better than this year's winners, and it is particularly encouraging to see so much new, young talent among them.'

I felt Louise's hand on my arm. 'That's you,' she mouthed silently, and I felt again that inner thrill I'd had when first I'd heard that I was a winner.

I looked around the room: at the elegantly-dressed guests, the linen tablecloths, the flowers on the tables, the display boards on which our work was now exhibited. I could see my pictures, overall winners in the 'Photo Story' category, and I thought of that day with Philippe.

They said it was 45°—50° most days but to be honest, once it went above 40° I couldn't really tell the difference. I just knew I felt permanently exhausted and my clothes stuck to me as if I'd been through the shower in them. I, who hardly ever drank water at home, could have drunk litre after litre but we had to be careful with our supply. There was enough for our needs, I'd been told, but not enough for us to be excessive or wasteful.

'Normally, back home, you'd probably lose between two and four litres of fluid a day, through exhalation and perspiration,' Philippe told me. 'Out here, with the very high temperatures, and the humidity, that amount will be more like ten to twenty litres, depending on how much you exert yourself. It's vital that you replenish that or you'll be no good to anyone.'

Philippe had worked previously with Médecins Sans Frontières for two years and knew what he was talking about.

'Let me know if you feel any signs of cramp, or begin to feel disorientated.'

'How can I not feel disorientated, when I'm suddenly whisked from the civilised comfort of West 6 and deposited on a dirt road in some God-forsaken part of Africa?'

Philippe tutted and shook his head: 'You know what I mean. Something more than a lack of familiarity with your surroundings. You'll be sure to tell me… don't worry that it might be a false alarm. We need to know.'

'Don't worry,' I replied. 'I'll tell you!'

The Land Rover rumbled and lurched over the rutted dirt road. Behind us lumbered the big lorry carrying our supplies but I could barely see it through the dustcloud thrown up by our wheels. Here and there lay the emaciated carcasses of dead animals—donkeys, I think, but it was hard to tell from the little that was left of them. On some the skins were stretched taut over rib cages and hip bones, whilst on others even the last traces of flesh and hide had been stripped off, leaving the blanched bones. I wondered what sort of creatures had been responsible. Vultures, maybe? Or maggots? Or maybe even starving people? I shuddered to think what desperate circumstances might bring someone to such a state.

I was aware of the smell some time before the camp was visible. It was hard to describe—the usual, almost spicy scent of the orange-red sand which made up the landscape, and with it a mixture of sweat, unwashed bodies, excrement and urine, together with a strong helping of necrosis. I was grateful when the driver and our interpreters lit their Arab cigarettes, drawing the acrid smoke deeply into their lungs and then exhaling from their nostrils blue streams which wafted over me as I struggled to stay on the narrow bench seat in the back.

'Nearly there now,' shouted Philippe above the growl of the diesel engine. 'Maybe you can tell?' and he gripped the end of his nose between his thumb and index finger.

I nodded.

'Once we get over the ridge, you'll see what it is that we're trying to cope with.'

Indeed I did, and I don't think anything could have prepared me adequately for it.

The Land Rover stopped at the top of the ridge and we got out. In front of us, the landscape fell away gradually but instead of the barren, empty desert through which we had been driving for most of the day, I saw a city. Oh, not a city of buildings and roadways, of houses and shops , such as I had left behind me in Britain, but a city of flimsy, ramshackle shelters, packed together in chaotic disorder as far as I could see into the distance. A thin haze hung over the whole site like a London fog, but through it I could make out a figure here and there moving slowly between the shelters.

'Good God!' I heard myself say.

'Yes,' Philippe responded, 'Good God. To bring us these thousands to try to feed and care for, to try to keep alive until whatever God or man may throw at them next. You'll pardon me if I can't get too enthusiastic in thanking Him!'

'I didn't mean…It's just an expression. Like "Mon Dieu!"'

'I know. But somehow God and this don't seem to go together.'

We got back into our vehicles and drove down the slope until we reached what served as a road between two sections of the settlement. Here the desperate state in which people were living was made all the more clear.

Many of the makeshift shelters were simple, dome-like constructions of sticks, with pieces of cloth and skins draped over them. Their shape gave them the appearance of the tops of lots of giant heads sticking up out of the parched ground. Others were made up of woven grass mats somehow supported against each other. I tried to imagine how they would be in a strong wind or heavy rain, should it come, and decided they would afford little shelter to the occupants.

In any space which had once been between the ramshackle dwellings, people without shelters had settled—almost as if they had just stopped, collapsed from exhaustion, maybe, too weary or hopeless to go any further. There they crouched or lay among their meagre belongings, the few pieces they had managed to salvage from their previous lives—a jumble of misshapen bundles—here a straw basket, there a cooking pot, or a plastic jerrican.

My expression must have revealed something of what I was thinking. Philippe was beside me, handing me my camera.

'Come on, then, Mr Media Man. Start shooting. You're gonna show the world what it's like to be living on the edge of disaster.'

I looked around me at the squalid dwellings, the pathetic figures squatting among them, their gaunt faces and staring, vacant eyes. Suddenly I realised the enormity of the task I had undertaken. How pompous of me to have thought that the few insignificant pieces I'd had accepted and published in the magazine could in any way have prepared me for this assignment!

'You're sure you're okay with this, Malcolm?' the features editor had asked me as we sat in her office overlooking the sweep of the Thames. 'Only it's rather different from your usual travel work.'

'I'm a photo-journalist, Louise, a visual reporter of news. I can handle it. After all, it's just people, places and situation, isn't it? I go there; I take my pictures, talk to a few people and soak up some of the local colour. No problem.'

'I think you'll find there's more to it than that.' She drew hungrily on her cigarette and blew a stream of smoke into the air above her. 'These aren't people who've gone to the region on holiday, you know, or chosen to be there. They're refugees, remember.'

'Right. Refugees. I know. I've seen news clips. It won't be a problem.'

Now, among the wretched squalor of the camp, I realised she had been right. You arrogant, ignorant bastard, I told myself. Twenty nine and you think you know life. Well, this'll teach you something you couldn't learn on a Thomas Cook tour.

I told myself I was a professional, reminded myself of what I had said to Louise, clenched my jaw against the smells, and set to work.

Accompanied by one of the interpreters I moved between the tents, my shutter clicking with every second. At most shelters the haggard occupants barely gave us a glance, but I came upon one particularly flimsy construction where what I saw stopped me in my tracks. Four pieces of branch, similar to what I remembered my grandmother using as a prop for her washing line, were placed into the ground and supported a thin lattice work roof of smaller branches, across which tattered grass matting had been placed. Beneath this meagre shelter sat a woman and five children. The oldest could not have been more than seven or eight by my reckoning, and the youngest, still an infant, she held loosely in her lap. Beside her a couple of empty cooking pots sat on the ashes of a long-dead fire.

It was the woman herself, or rather her position and what she was wearing, which had brought me to a halt. She was half reclining on the bare earth, legs bent at the knees, the child resting on them cradled in her right arm, and her left out to her side for support. She was dressed in a beautiful, flowing garment of the most vibrant orange, decorated with white and blue abstract designs. It was wrapped around her slender body, and from her right shoulder it looped behind and over her head before draping across her breast and over her outstretched arm. The fabric and the composition of the shot were almost identical to one I had taken in the Caribbean a few weeks before!

I had been assigned to do a feature on some of the lesser known islands and had found myself on Saint-Martin, an expensive getaway destination for the very rich in the French Caribbean. There on one of the beaches I had spotted a woman sitting under a sunshade of palm branches, a child resting in her lap. I took multiple photographs of her, one of which showed her with the sun reflecting on the sea behind her so that it looked like a halo. Later it had appeared in the magazine with the title "Madonna of Saint-Martin". She had been wearing a kaftan of almost exactly the design the refugee woman was now wearing, and was cradling her child in just the way this woman was cradling hers. Where my African subject had empty cooking pots, the beach woman had a picnic hamper and a bag of expensive sun creams.

Ignoring the other children who sat with her, I focused on the woman and her cradled child. It was uncanny how the composition mirrored the one I had taken in the Caribbean. All that was missing was the halo. I took dozens of shots in quick succession, adjusting my position slightly as I went in order to be sure that among them I got exactly the same angle as I had had in Saint-Martin. All the time the woman stared at me, expressionless and unmoving. When I thought I had enough pictures of her, we moved on, but my mind was no longer on the assignment. I couldn't wait to get back to London.

Louise had been pleased with my pictures, many of which appeared in a feature "The Plight of Africa" in one of the Sunday supplements. But I had kept back the shots of the woman.

In my studio I spent hours comparing the images of the idle holidaymaker on Saint-Martin with the destitute refugee, weighing each, carefully examining their expressions, the fall and drape of their clothing, the positions of their arms and of the child each cradled, until I was satisfied that I had as near perfect a match as I could achieve. The competition called for two sets of images illustrating the same story or event, and in effect telling a story in pictures. My submission included virtually matching pictures of the two women, together with additional prints highlighting the extremes of their lifestyles. The shot showing the Saint-Martin woman eating food from her picnic hamper was contrasted with the African woman's empty cooking pots. The well-nourished, sleeping child was juxtaposed with the swollen belly and emaciated body of the other. A close-up of the smiling lady from the Caribbean had its antithesis in the gaunt and desperate portrait of the refugee, while distance shots showed the idyllic setting of the Caribbean beach and the grim landscape of the refugee camp. Together they told a story of privilege and of deprivation. Without words they epitomized the gulf between the affluent west and the starving millions of Africa. They had won for me the 'Photo Story' award

Now, as Halliday announced the winners in the various categories, and presented the awards, I waited in the elegance of the ballroom for my big moment. Around the room the work of all the winners in the various categories was displayed. The most prominent feature was my work, entitled: "Witness and Interpret". I had based the title on something I remembered reading: "the photojournalist is a witness, an adventurer, and an interpreter of history". My work! Displayed for all to see and to admire! I savoured the experience. From the thousands of entries, people who had been in the business for years had chosen mine. In doing so they had acknowledged me as being right up there among the best. In a few minutes I would walk up onto that stage to receive the award, but more importantly for me, to receive the applause which we were now giving as each winner collected his prize. As recipient of the most prestigious award, I would be called as the last to receive the recognition of all my colleagues. They would probably stand to applaud me—perhaps even cheer. Photographs of me would be in the next day's papers: me collecting the trophy, me shaking hands with Russell Halliday, me smiling at the banks of news reporters, me giving the speech I had practised so long in front of the mirror. It felt good. I smiled to myself.

Louise leaned towards me and whispered. 'Why the smile? Something amusing you?'

'Just feeling rather pleased with myself. After all, it's quite an accolade for one's talent to be acknowledged publicly—especially at an affair like this and in such a venue. Don't you think?'

'True, Malcolm. You've done exceptionally well to receive it so young. You deserve it.'

I put my hand on hers. 'And I owe it all to you.'

'To me?'

'Of course. If you hadn't sent me out there, we wouldn't be sitting here now. I have you to thank for all this.' With a nod of my head I indicated the room, the columns, the beautifully draped curtains, the people in their evening dress.

Louise frowned. 'Aren't you forgetting someone?'

I thought for a moment. 'I don't think so. Who do you mean?'

'I was thinking of that poor African woman—and her starving children. Surely she's someone you should be thinking of? God knows I've thought enough about her since I first saw those awful photographs.'

I heard Russell begin introducing me. Adjusting my tie in readiness, I leaned towards Louise. 'Her? I think she's probably dead by now, don't you? And her children. They don't last long in the camps, you know.'

A spotlight had been directed towards our table and now, as I stood, the applause erupted around me.

'Clearly, I misjudged you, Malcolm. I thought your entry showed some compassion. I can't imagine how you could have been there and not felt some empathy for those poor people - identified with them in some way.'

'Identify with them? Louise, what on earth could they have which would make me identify with them?' I stretched out my hands and indicated the assembly. 'This is what I identify with. This is me. This is what I deserve.'

Suddenly she was on her feet beside me. 'You arrogant, insensitive bastard!' She grabbed our glasses from the table and flung the contents at me. As I stood with the red wine dripping from me, she slapped me around the face and stormed off. All around me, the photographers had a field day.

LENDAL MAY

Wilf Jones

Where peacocks prowl
The roofs and empty streets
And crack the morning
With impatient cry,
 make early birds of those
 who slept with windows wide
 this Spring-cum-Summer night by;

Where the dreaming and the waking
Meet between the sheets;

Where peals pre-matins joyous bell
And make the air expectant, full:
 they ring the River's swell;

Where swifts outrace the currents
Shrieking their delight;

Where soon behind the gap-tooth walls
The paying guest will stir,
 while tight within them
 those with wings make squabble;

All these to the rousing peacock cries
        will bring a flood of sound,
        a company in sound,
        full echo to the eye:

        Dawn to the Minster
        Sings the Glory!

An International Incident

Russell Kemp

I'm sitting here with a glass of brandy (for medicinal purposes only) on the balcony of an apartment in the centre of a large village on the Costa Tropical. It is approaching two p.m., the heat has risen well into the eighties and now that the Guardia Civil has left, and the clearing up from a little fracas of a couple of hours ago has been completed, the locals are winding down for the siesta.

In being so well located, Alice Sedgewick and I are ideally placed to observe the daily life of the population, which chiefly seems to consist of promenading up and down our street, loudly socialising with everybody they encounter.

If I may say so, Alice is not as worldly as myself, and I thought that bringing her to one of the Costa's would "bring her out" and help her to loosen up a bit, thereby enabling us to develop a more intimate relationship away from the stifling presence of her domineering mother. Naturally at this stage of our relationship we are still occupying separate bedrooms.

This morning being our first in the village, we decided to explore the delights of the local market, which is held on this day, every week. It really is quite extensive, overflowing from the large plaza into several narrow side streets. We wandered through the usual array of clothes stalls, agricultural produce, leather goods and the like, until we came upon a portrait artist, proudly displaying vibrant examples of his work. All of which, in truth I have to say, bore an uncanny resemblance to Victoria Beckham. Not that I imply any criticism of Mrs Beckham, I hasten to add. With all the charm of a hungry alligator he seized upon Alice, and apparently being so deeply affected by her beauty, offered to encapsulate it on one of his canvases as a special favour to me—for fifty euros. Alice not being as sophisticated as myself, did not realise that no slight was intended when I started to haggle at twenty. As a result of her ensuing pique, Picasso and myself never finalised negotiations because she flounced off into a pasteleria just across the street, and regardless of my concerns about her figure, bought a large bocadillo. Alice is one of those women, who after bearing a couple of children, will balloon to size twenty or more!

From there on, events rapidly spun out of control. Hardly had I left Picasso's side, when a dark-skinned young man with shades in his hair, and nattily dressed in a crisp shirt and chinos, (Alice continues to describe him as handsome) appeared in front of me.

'Good morning, sir,' he started off, 'have you ever considered buying a time share?' One glance at the pamphlets in his hand told me all I needed to know. It is a very foolish person indeed who walks unprepared into Johnny Foreigner's backyard, and my first reaction was to ignore him.

'How would you feel about coming to view one of our nice air-conditioned properties and enjoying a glass of wine?' he persisted. 'There's no obligation to buy.'

Clearly this approach was not working, so I deployed plan B, which I had cunningly devised before leaving for foreign climes.

'Himmel, mein Gott, Brunhilde! Eine Vorsprung durch Techniker!' I shouted stridently at the returning Alice. The effect of this was exhilarating, everything went quiet, the scene took on a freeze-frame quality as all eyes focused on me. Even the Spanish stopped talking. Flushed with success I continued with the only other piece of German that I could bring to mind.

'Haben Sie ein Schlafzimmer frie?' I demanded of my tormentor.

'Schweinherde!' exploded somebody to my right, 'you insulted meine frau!'

Well I hadn't, but regrettably, there was no time for denials. I ducked instinctively as a fist attached to a red-faced, blond man whizzed past and struck the face of the salesman. The salesman was a game little fellow, and after extracting himself from the wreckage of Picasso's display, rushed forward and smashed a large likeness of Victoria Beckham over his assailant's head. Brunhilde, clearly enraged at the sight of her husband's head protruding from Mrs B's cleavage, snatched up a large earthenware flagon of olive oil from a handily placed display and, with a flick of her magnificent torso, she hurled it at both Picasso and the salesman.

'Was it Extra Virgin?' you may be wondering. For all I know it may well have been, but in the circumstances I was not going to risk a misunderstanding, if you follow my drift.

The flagon burst spectacularly against the wall above Picasso's palette, showering a mixture of paint and oil everywhere. Picasso, seething with anger, now threw himself across the street at Brunhilde. The stallholder, rushing to claim reimbursement, slipped and fell, thereby knocking a further five people into the mire. Some unresolved local issues may have resurfaced here, as the indigenous population, sensing that this was too good an opportunity to miss, all too willingly rounded on the tourists.

Alice and I wanted no part of this, and seeking deliverance, took refuge in the nearby chapel of Our Lady of The Annunciation. In recognition of the gravity of the situation, we lit a candle to St Christopher. The Holy Father, no doubt impressed by our piety, beckoned us over to the communion rail and asked us to join him in a prayer for "World Peece." Outside the battle raged for several minutes more as he rambled on and on. We had no idea what he was saying—it was all Greek to us. Eventually, the wailing of many sirens brought an end to hostilities, and the priest returned to the real world, noting with distaste the half-eaten bocadillo in Alice's hand. We walked in awkward silence back to the entrance. Opening the great wooden door, the penitent holy-man looked out and surveyed the devastation. With an air of defeat and resignation he rolled his eyes to the skies and muttered, 'Santa Maria! Ever since the Engleesh arrive!'

As I hope you can appreciate, I was stunned by this slanderous indictment of our fellow countrymen, and by a man of the cloth as well! My ire was roused, I was about to point out to him that this disturbance was caused by a Spaniard and a German, when Alice shoved the remains of her snack into my opening mouth.

'Leave it, Fred,' she hissed, in a manner horribly similar to that of her mother. 'You've said enough today already!'

Alice says she just hopes that nobody down there is looking for us.

LIFE FOR A LIFE

Jo Marsh

This is a story, so they say.

My big brothers were intellectually younger than me. When the light submitted to the dark, they—my brothers and my father—returned and transformed the family home into a house, a hotel, a nightclub and a launderette. Testosterone filled the air. My mother retreated to her sewing room. I escaped to the copse on the far edge of the horizon, my bolt hole, my oxygen tank, my safe haven.

I left the city early to avoid delay. My father had been specific about the arrangements: it was paramount that I was not late for my youngest brother Tom's surprise party. Upon arrival I would be met at the station and must not ring the house. I was to wait until he came for me.

I was travelling down from Liverpool, where I was a student at the university—a world apart from my real life. My family had said it would be the making of me; instead it made me think of the ingredients of a cake, my father the sour milk.

The bustling platform disappeared. The window frame, in breaking my view, reminded me of one of those childhood toys that move so fast it makes the static pictures look as if they are moving. The only reason you know it's not a movie is because there are fault lines; if you look carefully you can see where the images don't line up.

The train tacked efficiently between the high rise tower blocks, momentarily dipping below the surface before re-emerging; neither missed in its absence, nor noticed in its presence. Industry changed to housing, changed to fields, changed to valleys. Travellers got off, and got on, and got off and got on. Time passed slowly. When the darkness masked the exterior view I focussed on the interior: three public school boys, distinctive in their schoolboy suit of blazers, ties and scarves, little men in training, scuffling, mocking, teasing; a mum with a buggy turned to face the grey wall of the carriage, away from the risk of contamination from an adulterated world; a couple opposite who bubbled with excitement, they had boarded separately and exchanged no more than a snapshot glance in the others' direction, although the woman's sudden flush confirmed my suspicions—yet who was I to judge?

The train slowed. A silent boy and I stared into the blackness. As we drew into the remote station the lamps on the platform exposed the shadow of my father waiting. I had coveted childhood memories of me and mum and Samuel, memories that played out on the inside of my closed eyelids over and over again.

The last time I had seen my mum her eyesight had been failing. She said it was as if she lived in a monochrome world with the lights turned out. She had been offered eye surgery which, although not always the answer, was successful in enough cases to be worth trying. My father had objected. He disputed the need for my mum to see more than she was able, claiming it was a waste of health service resources. He argued there were more worthwhile cases that could benefit from the money her operation would cost. He had been persistently forceful, which was the only way he knew, but Mum went ahead anyway and her last letter had said the operation was successful. The monochrome effect had transformed into an artist's palette with her levels of visual clarity improving steadily.

Three small steps down from the train seemed to me to be a longer journey than the four hours from Liverpool. I stood, a composed twenty year-old, eyes wide, one hand twisting a ragged tissue in my pocket, the other keeping my coat closed. As I took tiny paces towards the unmoving shadow of my father, the sound of a whistle shot up in the air, dragging my heart with it. Having twisted to watch the train retreat, I turned back. The shadow had shifted. My heart leapt against the force of my father's hands as they steadied me, tight on my arms. I knew the rote: arms, hug, car. To the absent onlooker we would be a normal father and daughter. I released the child locks as I climbed in. The journey back to the family home was stifled in silence.

The spinning top was beginning to slow.

As we pulled into the drive I noticed my childhood home was different now. It used to look as though it belonged in a fairground, with windows on different levels and shapes that shifted mechanically behind them. The floorboards creaked and moved. Things touched you—slow, creeping, invasive things. School friends would come back for tea sometimes, and usually only visited once, politely declining further invitations. It had not been long before my home had been renamed "The House of Horrors."

Things had changed though. Ragged strips of fabric no longer tussled in the breeze. In their place hung modern wooden blinds pulled open to the top—the house stared back at us, seeing, accusing, questioning. Although the windows were not symmetrical, ornaments, chosen for their size and shape, balanced the image. The large windows were adorned with small jugs and small windows with large vases; everything fitted in a way that it had not before. The darkness no longer forced its way inside. Instead, the house wrestled back, constraining the encroaching darkness and forcing the light from inside, outside. Former shadows had lost their hiding places.

My middle brother, Samuel, momentarily darkened the shadow on the lawn, and as he realised our father was not alone he lurched towards the car. He powered the front door open and, pulling me away from the car, held me by the shoulders. The familiarity coursed through me as he leant back and our eyes locked. While everything around us swirled, captured by the stillness at the centre of the vortex, fifteen years of apologies, explanations and promises were silently exchanged. A different hand on my back, lighter, gentler, joined in the reunion.

'Mum, oh Mum,' I said, 'so good to see you.'

'No love, good to see you.'

We laughed, joyous, shameless, laughter. Wrapped around each other, a slightly unbalanced body of people, we walked back to the house.

Being home felt good, but there was one other place I needed to see. I knew it would have to wait however; for now I would hold my breath.

Sandwiches, crisps, balloons, clearing furniture, laying tables and answering the phone filled the hours that followed. Just moments before Tom arrived the last banner was hung in place. Anticipating one of my father's curries, Tom juggled two bottles of mulberry red wine as his key slid comfortably into the lock. Tom had always delighted in my father's tastes in a way neither Samuel or I could appreciate. Having writhed into the tiniest of spaces, I now joined in the communal cry of 'Surprise!' Tom's unspoken greeting—the fleeting motion of muscles that tensed below and above his eyes—spoke more of anxiety.

The spinning top faltered slightly before righting itself.

Party poppers screamed, lights dimmed, corks multiplied

silently. I circulated, mingled, laughed, listened and hosted. For the first time in a long time, our family was as it had been. By the early hours, only Tom's closest friends were left, all set in where they would sleep and beyond noticing my departure. The blinds that had witnessed my arrival were now at rest. With the light from inside withheld by the wooden slats, my exit into the shadows was mutely absorbed. I had one last place to go—my bolt hole, my oxygen tank.

My eyes quickly adjusted to the blackness as I made my way to the retreat on the horizon. Gulping deeply I felt euphoric on air. I resented the fact that I would only have a few short hours here. The shelter, built from scraps, resembled an oversized ghost in the darkness. Three sides were made from old fence panels, the roof a large waterproof sheet. As a child I had spent whole days here. Nobody had ever questioned why or where I'd been.

Here, the air no longer seemed so crisp, and before I saw it, I smelt a fire burning. Orange light and flickering shadows played on the tree trunks. As I rounded the third side of the structure I saw him: my father, an unwanted squatter, brooding and erect—a monstrous shape. I had no idea how long he had lain in wait. Nauseated, I lurched against the shelter. This was my place, not his. Fifteen long years had taught me there was no point in screaming, nobody ever heard anything out here. He lunged, striking me to the ground. Horizontal I focused only on the fire. Through it I saw again the bed legs, the dolls, the train sets and once, my brother's unmoving feet, his trouser bottoms quivering as urine slowly puddled at his feet. He fell on me, all fourteen stone of him, crushing the air from my lungs, forcing, pushing, a car with the accelerator jammed; he was unrelenting. He thrust again and again, grunting with the effort, guttural, ragged. I could only imagine his face contorted with revulsion—at me, at him.

The fire pulsed with heat, dying down before reviving,

over and over. Young wood smothered beneath the weightier older branches; kindling incinerated by the fire turned to dust. Dust to dust, ashes to ashes. A living death. I watched him walk away. I watched him walk.

That night the spinning-top toppled, stopped, and broke.

I watched him. I watched.

Abuse was not a word in the valley-dwellers' vocabulary, they did not want to believe, to think it possible. Nobody could do that to somebody they loved. But that was my point: because they loved, they did it.

A story, so they say.

They had known my father, Matt, and his father before him. I was accused of casting shadows on the family. They did not want to hear it, they would not hear it.

My life had already been sacrificed. I stood only to gain from my decision. I kept the baby. I knew, throughout the pregnancy, there could be problems. The baby needed treatment and the hospital tested all my relatives: blood, stem-cells, organs.

My mum cried when she first saw Alfie. My father too, but not in the same way: hers had been selfless tears of pity. The tests had to be done quickly. I would have preferred a creeping painful process—he deserved nothing less. The hospital staff closed doors, shutting us out. Then the day came when they invited me into their safe haven; the day I had waited for, so many years. I turned to my mum for support. Only then did she see the torture in my face. They knew, they could tell from the test results—the similarities were too close for coincidence. I told them: it was no coincidence. My mum wept angry, apologetic tears.

I watched my father, handcuffed, escorted away. I watched him walk away.

HATTERALL HILL

Laura Haines

(Written when walking in the Brecon Beacons.)

Cuckoo spit like snowflakes beneath
The larks' bubbling call.
Llanthony's stone arches whisper
Secrets, that kept us down in the valley shade.
From up here, I could prop up the tower with
One finger. God's walls
So perfectly made.

Recycling

Julian Corbell

I love car boot sales and delight in finding real bargains for me and my children, sometimes even for my sister, though I have to be careful with her as she has a preference for new things at full price. It's a two-way thing with me as well—I often go to sell rather than to buy, finding great satisfaction in unloading my used-up toys and baby clothes on others. This morning I was just buying, looking for something really cheap and useful. Among the enormous number of stalls laid out across the field that sunny Sunday morning, there was one that stood out as different. It just looked somehow sadder than the others. I had already walked quickly past several dozen portable tables, glancing at each collection with no special interest, until this one made me pause. It wasn't so much the items that were special, rather the person selling them. She looked really unhappy, whereas most other hopeful sellers were quite upbeat, cheerful and outgoing. This woman was withdrawn in her bodily stance, yet well-dressed, both aspects marking her out as a "first-timer". In spite of her uneasy manner, she still faced up to the crowds of passers-by, wanting to sell, yet unwilling to make the first move. Having paused to look at her, I lowered my gaze to the items in front of her.

There was a display of crockery that looked very old, yet

well cared for, and almost opulent with its traditional blue design and gold-leaf edging. Crockery generally changed hands for less than £1, yet these plates looked expensive. Had the woman fallen on really hard times? Next to the plates were several electronic toys, the sort of item I am generally cautious about, because they often fail to work in the way the designer intended, due to enthusiastic childish mishandling. Beside the table, in a forlorn space all to itself, was the object that caught my attention most of all, since I had recently given birth to my fourth child, and needed one of these. It was a folding push-chair with several of the useful extras I could also use, such as a car-seat and a water-proof cover. One glance was enough to tell me it would sell for over £300 when new. This one looked hardly used.

'How much?' I said, pointing.

'Thirty pounds,' answered the woman, stepping forward slightly and placing her fingers tenderly onto the handle. 'It's in very good condition. Hardly used.' She paused, her voice faltering. Then taking a deep breath, and swallowing hard, she added 'Is it for you?'

'Could be,' I said. 'I wasn't expecting to need one again, but, you know…'

'Yes, I do.' She paused again, perhaps wanting to tell me more, but not daring to start. 'Why don't you have a proper look?' As she spoke, she pushed the chair towards me, looking not at me but at the chair seat, as if there were a child in it to be admired. I took it from her, knowing she could ask far more than £30, but still ready to barter.

'Will you accept £20?' I ventured, ready for a few minutes' enjoyable negotiation.

'No, I have to have £30,' she said quickly and quite firmly. Then she softened and added: 'That's the price my daughter gave me and I said I would stick to it.'

'She kept it in excellent condition. She must have cleaned

it far more often than I usually do. Is the car-seat included in the price?'

'Yes it is. And it's clean because she...she only needed it for two weeks. There, I was trying not to talk about it, but how can I not?' She looked away and groped for a hanky.

'I'm sorry,' I said, still holding the push-chair. 'Don't upset yourself. You don't need to tell me.'

She stared at me over her hanky for quite some time, blowing her nose and sniffing, appearing to be having a debate with herself about how to move on.

'You look understanding and sympathetic,' she finally said. 'And you've got children, so you'll know. My daughter...' She paused again, blinking and swallowing hard, holding firmly to the table. 'My daughter had just had her first baby, my first grandson, when both the child and his father were killed in a car crash. We just can't bear to look at anything that reminds us of them. I must sell it, the toys as well. I expect they were quite unsuitable, far too old for a baby, but, you know, I was thinking of the future.'

I stared at her for a moment, then at the ground. 'I'm so sorry. This must be very difficult for you, coming here with all these people.'

'I'm finding it actually helps, seeing all of life around me going on in spite of my grief. My daughter couldn't possibly have come. She's still in shock, hardly able to cope at the moment.'

I smiled at her, admiring her courage, and wondering what else she might share with me. Another couple with two children approached.

'How much for the crockery?' said the man. 'It looks pretty old, can't be worth much.'

'It is old, and is therefore worth a lot,' she said precisely, 'but I'm asking £10 for the set.'

'£10! No way! I'll give you two quid.'

'I must have £10,' she replied, standing up straighter and looking at the woman next to him. 'You could serve the Queen with these. They are worth far more, but if I get £10 this morning I shall be satisfied.'

'Nah, far too much. Come on Sylv, there's more over there.' And they moved on. I was still standing with my hand on the push-chair, already feeling it was mine. But the plates puzzled me.

'Why are you selling the plates?' I ventured, feeling she was almost a friend now. 'They are beautiful, and much older than either of us, I expect.'

'Yes, over 100 years old, passed down to my late son-in-law as a wedding present. His mother, who gave them, is now dead, and my daughter can't look at them without sobbing, so I said I would bring them here, get the best price I could, and then we'll see. I know you won't want them, but how about one of these toys for your other children? They've never been touched, still under guarantee, with fresh batteries. £2 each. I can see you're more used to this than I am, but that must be the bargain of the day. I just want to sell them and go home.'

'It might be your first day here, but you're good at it!' I said. 'I'll take the push-chair, and the three toys, then each of my children has something to be pleased with.' As I counted out the money onto the table, I was right next to the plates. She was right, they were wonderful. My eldest daughter was bound to marry soon, if only to fend off some of the less favourable boyfriends. What a wonderful wedding present they would make!

The Home of Santa Claus

Barry Baddock

It was the landlord's idea. He suddenly decided to invite all his tenants to share a spot of seasonal goodwill. But Dr Meier himself didn't live on the premises. He conducted his grand property speculations from a turreted villa in the hills. So it was the resident Hausmeister—poor old Herr Wilke— who was coerced into hosting the little gathering.

It was a painful half-hour.

Dr Meier loudly aired his views on the question of the Russian immigrants, stressing each labyrinthine sentence with a flailing arm. His listeners, holding thin-stemmed glasses of champagne, stood ponderous and rigid, like convicts packed in a cell. One man did venture to speak, but the landlord wheeled on him—*Mein lieber Herr Blockwitz!*—and strode into a new tirade about integration.

Old Herr Wilke plodded back and forth, offering Sekt and tiny sandwiches to the dismal audience.

As Dr Meier threaded his way through another ghastly Teutonic construction, I fell to staring at objects around me. Herr Wilke's potted plants. Lumps of black mahogany. A suitcase-sized Grundig radio, bearing the names of ancient transmitters: München, Hilversum, Wien. On it stood a large card, painted by a child. It showed four red reindeer floating above a spread-eagled Santa Claus. *Schöne Weihnachten aus*

LAPPLAND. A happy Christmas from Lapland. The big letters dangled in a bold variety of colours.

I found Herr Wilke at my side. Careful not to disturb Dr Meier's drone, he whispered to me that his great granddaughter had made the card. I nodded and smiled.

Peering at me shyly, he conveyed more: she was just eight years old and her name was Karin. The old man seemed genuinely glad that someone had taken an interest in her work. At the same time, I think he had latched onto me because he was out of his depth among the intense company.

Dr Meier's harangue ended abruptly. Next thing, he was shaking hands, nodding farewells and barking into his mobile phone. No sooner had the good Doctor sped off than the surreal gathering melted away entirely.

Truth to tell, I was set to leave too, but Herr Wilke blocked my path. A slab-like photo album was in his hands.

With quiet pleasure, he showed me photos of various stations in his great granddaughter's young life. Then, by and by, we moved to older pictures. Family groups in sepia. Jolly youths boating on a lake. A wedding couple. Herr Wilke's late wife. His father, a vintner in Würzburg, with Tyrolean hat and Kaiser moustache. And Herr Wilke's brother, Gerd, in infantry uniform. He stood with his back to the family vineyard, smiling the blushing smile of the Wilkes.

Was Gerd still alive, I asked? No. Gerd fell into Russian hands on the Eastern front and spent long years as a prisoner of war. Then, shortly after his release and return to Germany, he died.

Wie schrecklich, I murmured. How terrible.

Herr Wilke sat gazing at the picture for a moment, then closed the album.

Ist alles vorbei, he said. It's all past.

He nodded to the Christmas card again. Lapland was in Finland, he explained. Looking sideways, with that odd bashful smile, he said Lapland was the home of Santa Claus. Little Karin had painted the card just for him, because she knew he had been there.

Das ist wunderbar, I said.

He misunderstood me. *Ja, Lappland ist wunderbar. Kristallweiss.* As white as crystal. In Lapland, he explained, the land and the sky and the forest were one. Crystal-white. And there were red reindeer, like those in his great granddaughter's card.

Herr Wilke's choice of schnaps was a purplish blend of cough mixture and pig's bile. At the first taste, I screwed up my face at him.

Bitter im Mund, im Herzen gesund, he announced cheerfully. Bitter to the taste, healthy for the heart. Then he swallowed more of the vile stuff.

Every day that nation brought something new to amaze me. At some dark, harsh period of German history, schnaps must have killed off the weaklings and left only the fittest survivors, a Volk with guts of steel. There were millions like Herr Wilke, immune to gastroenteritis, who could swill down such poison with no damaging effect.

I sipped more of the purple venom. Then, a little stupefied, I sat and gazed at the winsome picture of Santa Claus in Lapland. Kristallweiss…

Lights flashed in my brain and wheels began to turn.

I asked my host when he had been in Lapland.

He blinked. *Im Krieg*, he said. In the War. With his artillery division. They were stationed in northern Finland, fighting against the Soviets, alongside the Finns. Until the division received the order to pack up and make the long trek to Norway – then they had to march by night and bivouac in the forest by day, to hide from the Russians.

Vor der Russen, Herr Wilke repeated. He held my eyes for a second, then poured himself another glass of schnaps. He offered me the bottle. But I shook my head. And waited.

Pensively, he opened the album again. He turned the pages until he found several tiny pictures of uniformed men in snow.

*Das ist Leutnant Barth, das ist Leutnant Klages...*he named them all, with the coy pleasure of a schoolboy showing off his form prizes. *Da bin ich*. There I am.

One picture showed a soldier arm in arm with a young woman, at the gate of a snow-covered wooden house. They smiled at the camera in their greatcoats and fur hats.

Bernd und Eva, said Herr Wilke. Eva was from Lapland. They were engaged to be married after the War.

Did they marry?

No, Bernd died near Tornio during the retreat. Killed in a Russian mortar attack.

I waited. But that was all Herr Wilke had to say. *Ist alles vorbei.*

In my schnaps-induced haze, I strove to marshal my thoughts. Foremost among them was the knowledge that I was a guest in the man's home, and a foreign one at that. So I could not possibly ask the questions which were racing in my head.

In 1944, Finland changed sides and threw in their lot with the Russians. The German forces repaid the treachery with interest. In their retreat to the safety of the Norwegian border, they burned every home and every village in their wake. Mile by mile, they devastated the entire north of the country. It was a "scorched earth" operation of appalling ruthlessness.

Bridges were blown up, roads mined, telephone lines obliterated and almost half of all dwellings destroyed. The provincial capital, Rovaniemi, burned for six days. When the evacuated civilian population returned to Lapland, 100,000 of them found their homes laid to waste.

The man's quiet pride, his precise talk of comrades and field stations and infantry engagements...had Artilleryman Wilke forgotten the part he had played in the long horror?

Yes, he had. I am sure he had. No memory remained of petrol-doused homes, of the lighted torch and storming flames, or of grey wood-smoke billowing above ruins. *Ist alles vorbei.*

Atonement is bitter to the taste, healthy for the heart. But a terrible, unrequited deed is a monster at rest. It must not be hauled from its dark ravine, for that way lie madness and despair.

We shook hands, Herr Wilke and I, and bade each other a happy Christmas. And I left him, an old man, with his album, standing alone among potted plants and fusty black mahogany. And living a long-ago adventure in the manly uniform of the Reich, in a place, crystal-white, where land and sky and forest are one, and a monster hides.

DULCIMER

Wilf Jones

By the cold black rails of All Saints' he plays
And hails the city with his song:
The ancient walls, echoing round
The golden notes,
In joy resound.
All magic struck
The delicate, dancing motes abound,
Bring sunlit warmth
To Winter streets,
Bring to all a dream unfound
In life; will change this drab,
This cold, this weary college town,
As if the heart of Raphael
Came down
And blessed with skill
The busker's ageing hand,
And blesséd music, pure,
Poured like molten silver through,
And up, and all around,
And chased the streets with beauty.
And weary ears of Town and Gown,
Battered by their day,
Wake now! Wake now!

Wake now as the song,
Reclaims this frozen ground,
With flowers bright as Springtime air;
Now all who hear must praise the sound
Of Heaven's Dolcimelo.

The Cave of the Drunken Prince

Lisa Climie

He had called his apartment: 'The Cave of the Drunken Prince.' I smiled the first time I heard it and was drawn in. Later, as I heard him repeat that well-worn line to so many others, I felt cheated. The words had grown stale and tired in time, as had he.

No longer did they swarm to hear his tales of Warhol, his part in Andy's 15 minutes of fame, the stories of Studio 54.

'Johnny be good, Johnny be good!' they'd chorused as he held court at the bar.

'No, I'm Johnny too bad,' he'd reply in his lazy southern drawl before launching into another performance. I was captured, along with all the other fresh young things.

'I'll never forget Warren's face when I said, "Sorry honey, can't let you in."' he continued. 'Don't look so hard-done-by, baby. Why, I didn't even let Woody in or lil' ol' Frank. Yeah, Old Blue Eyes may have done it his way, but not at the 54 on opening night he didn't.'

He would laugh loud and hard, throwing back his head, hair in a tangle.

Bowing forwards he'd run his fingers through those golden locks, so when he looked up again the curls fell perfectly around his cherubic face. His deep blue eyes flashed with pleasure as they met our wide-eyed attention.

He was hooked to the attention as much as all the drugs and booze he consumed—and of course the sex.

Spotting his prey for the night: me, my innocence sparkling, attracting him by its pure light, he moved in for the kill. 'I was singin' with Liza, top of the bar: "New York, New York!" So loaded I could hardly stand.'

'Tell them about Bianca,' yelled a voice in the crowd.

'Don't think I'll ever help a naked lady gittup on a horse again! Not ever' day you're cheek to cheek with Bianca's butt. She rode in 'cross the dance floor; it was knee high in glitter. I just headed for the coke stash, waited while she finished so I could strut my stuff: Saturday Night Fever. Move over girlfriend, Johnny's here now!' He waved a dismissive hand and laughed again.

By then he had me firmly in his grip. Like being caught in a honey trap, I swooned to the smell of his sweet breath.

Like Johnny and so many others, I had come to the place where I thought I belonged, where I could be myself for the first time and dare to dream, free at last from those who couldn't understand, who disapproved. Free to love.

Yes, those were golden days.

Sex was liberating and fun and abundant. Cocaine—not addictive, they said—was everywhere for the taking. There was even love too, if you were lucky.

And then it came, silent and deadly, tearing a swathe through our number; none of us knowing what it was, or why it chose so many. I wasn't one of the first but I watched as one after another they fell, like nine-pins at a fair. Johnny too: his face grew thin, he covered up the marks with make-up. His strong beautiful body turned weak, his blood black and whispery in his veins. Where was the laughter then, Johnny? No time left for laughing, just fear-fed tears when no one was around. He still tried to use his charm, but now it seemed just predatory. It wasn't that he ever wanted to hurt anyone, but he did, over and over. I know he came to hate himself; he couldn't bear to be alone, couldn't bear to look at what he had become.

Now, as I watch, his blood running hot and fast, then slowing to a trickle, the smell acrid, strong, is overwhelming. I sit and I wait. I look at his hair, greying at the roots, lying limp and sweat sodden. His body grows cold and hard. Outside winter air freshens for snow. Waiting for the police to come, I stroke his brow and I whisper: 'Sleep now, sweet drunken prince, sleep now.'

Are Squirrels Clergy?

Tony Irvin

The girl held the man's hand as they crossed the park. 'Why did those boys call you a stupid old git, Grandad?' she asked.

'Probably because I told them off.'

'It's not very nice to throw stones at ducks, is it?'

'It's not very nice to call someone a stupid old…'

'Can we go and feed the ducks, Grandad?'

'Let's have a rest first, Lucy.'

'Why do you want a rest, Grandad? Are you feeling tired?'

'I'd just like a bit of a sit-down.'

'Oh, all right. Grandad, no! You can't sit there! You'll sit on Basil.'

'Basil?'

'Basil's sitting there. He got to the bench before us and just scrambled up, but I'll ask him to make room for you. Basil, can you move up and make room for Grandad. There, now you can sit down, Grandad. Basil says there's room for all of us.'

'Thank you, Basil. Ah, that's better.'

'Grandad, say hello to Basil.'

'Hello, Basil.'

'Basil, Grandad needs a bit of a rest. Basil says he understands, Grandad. He says you're just like Floppy.'

'Who's Floppy?'

'He's my rabbit; he's always having a rest. He's got this great big run but all he does is sit in one corner, 'cept when I go and give him dandelions, then he runs all over the place. He likes dandelions.'

'And I'm like Floppy?'

'Do you like dandelions, Grandad?'

'Not much.'

'Floppy's getting quite old. I 'spect that's why he likes sitting around.'

'Yes, you're probably right, Lucy.'

'You're quite old, aren't you, Grandad?'

'Well I'm not that…'

'Basil says old people need to rest more, 'cos they get worn out easy.'

'Yes, well…'

'Grandad, are you very old?'

'No, Lucy; I'm not very old.'

'You look really old.'

'Well, I probably look old to you, Lucy, but I certainly don't feel old.'

'So why do you want to have a rest?'

'I just thought it would be nice to…'

'How old are you, Grandad?'

'Lucy, you shouldn't ask people how old they are.'

'Why not?'

'Because it's rude, and they might get upset.'

'People are always asking me how old I am, and I tell them I'm five. I don't mind.'

'That's different.'

'Why's it different?'

'Well, they…'

'Next time someone asks me how old I am, I'll tell them it's rude to ask so I'm not saying.'

'The thing is, Lucy, with children no one minds asking…'

'Basil doesn't think it's rude to ask someone how old they are. Do you, Basil? Basil says it's not rude to ask.'

'All right, Lucy, you can tell Basil that I'm seventy-four.'

'Basil, Grandad is seventy-four. Basil says that's nearly as old as an elephant; they can live to seventy or eighty.'

'Is that so? Did I tell you I once saw an elephant in my pyjamas?'

'I know, Grandad, and you always wondered why he was in your pyjamas.'

'Have I told you that one before?'

'Lots of times.'

'Oh.'

'Grandad, when you die will you go to heaven?'

'I hope so, Lucy.'

'I won't go to heaven when I die.'

'Lucy, of course you will!'

'No, I won't, 'cos I called Millie a slug, and Miss Nicholls said that was very wicked, and I know wicked people don't go to heaven.'

'I don't think calling someone a slug is very wicked.'

'Miss Nicholls does, and she's our teacher. She says good people go to heaven and bad people go to the other place. So, I'll be going to the other place.'

'No, Lucy, you may have called Millie a slug because you were cross, but I'm sure you didn't mean it.'

'I jolly well did! She said my ears stuck out, but she's got these sticky-out eyes, like they're on stalks, that's why I said she looked like a slug, 'cos they've got eyes on stalks. 'Cept that's not slugs, that's snails, but I still called Millie a slug 'cos I don't s'pose she knows the difference. Basil also called her a slug, so he won't go to heaven either.'

'Let's not worry too much about that at the moment, Lucy, it'll be a long time before…'

'Grandad, where is heaven?'

'Goodness me, your questions. I don't know, Lucy.'

'But Mummy says you've travelled everywhere; you must know.'

'Well, I used to travel a lot before I retired.'

'So you must know where heaven is.'

'No, Lucy; we only find that out after we die.'

'Is it a long way away?'

'I expect so.'

'Is it near Guildford?'

'Guildford!'

'That's a long way away; it took us ages when we went to see Uncle Tim.'

'No, Lucy, I don't think heaven is near Guildford. Some people think that heaven is all around us, but no one really knows.'

'Is the other place near Guildford?'

'What other place?'

'The place where bad people go when they die.'

'No, that's not near Guildford either.'

'Oh well, it must be near Hendon, then.'

'Why on earth should it be near Hendon?'

'Cos Hendon and heaven sound the same.'

'They sound similar, but just because they sound similar, it doesn't mean they're near each other.'

'I was sick at Hendon. I threw up all over Daddy's car. It was 'cos I ate too many sweets, but Daddy said it was really Mummy's fault 'cos she kept giving them to me. Basil agreed with Daddy, didn't you Basil? Basil says it was Mummy's fault.'

'Was Basil sick as well?'

'Grandad, you mustn't tease.'

'Sorry.'

'We had to open all the windows 'cos of the pong, but I didn't mind 'cos it was my sick and you don't mind so much if it's your own...'

86

'I think that's enough, Lucy. Shall we talk about something else?'

'All right. Grandad?'

'What?'

'Do squirrels like duck food?

'I've no idea; why do you ask?'

'Cos there's a squirrel over there and he's looking at me. He's prob'ly thinking: I wonder what she's got in that bag.'

'Why don't you try? I think squirrels eat most things.'

'Do they eat sausages?'

'I don't suppose they'd be very keen on sausages, I think they prefer...'

'I meaned cold sausages. I know squirrels wouldn't like hot sausage 'cos they'd burn their mouths, and they wouldn't like bacon and eggs and fish fingers and...'

'I think squirrels prefer nuts and things like that.'

'Darren can't eat nuts.'

'Who's Darren?'

'He's a boy at our school – he's clergy.'

'He has an allergy?'

'That's what I said. He goes all red in the face and can't breathe if he has nuts.'

'Poor chap.'

'One day he ate some cake that had nuts in and Miss Nicholls had to call the ambulance and the ambulance came and its blue light was flashing and the men had yellow and green coats on and they put this mask thing on Darren's face and Miss Nicholls wouldn't let us look 'cos she said we shouldn't be nosy 'bout other people being ill. But she was looking, so I looked, and he was back at school next day.'

'Allergies can be like that; they come on very quickly but they can...'

'Are squirrels clergy?'

'No, I don't think so.'

'So the bread we've brought for the ducks would be all right?'

'Throw him a piece; if he rolls onto his back and waves his legs in the air, he's probably allergic.'

'Grandad, that's mean! Anyway, I'm going to give him a piece. There you are, Mr Squirrel.'

'Well, he seemed to like that, and he hasn't come to any harm.'

'I'm not giving him anymore, 'cos he might be a bit clergy and I want to save the rest for the ducks.'

'Good idea.'

'Are badgers clergy, Grandad?'

'No, I don't think so.'

'What about foxes and rabbits and hedgehogs and… and elephants?'

'Gracious, Lucy, how do you expect me to know? I suppose some animals might be allergic to certain foods, particularly if you gave them something they're not used to…'

'Grandad, what are those two people doing?'

'Which two people?'

'Those two lying over there on the grass.'

'They're kissing.'

'That's a funny way to kiss. You don't kiss lying down.'

'No, well… Shall we go and feed the ducks now?'

'Are they making a baby?'

'No, of course they're not; they're just kissing.'

'Miss Nicholls says you can make babies by kissing, but I kissed Darren once and I didn't make a baby.'

'You don't make babies like that.'

'Miss Nicholls says you do.'

'Perhaps, when… if, she becomes a Mrs she'll be in for a surprise.'

'What does that mean, Grandad?'

'Never mind, Lucy, you'll learn about these things when

you're older.'

'When I'm as old as you?'

'No, well before then.'

'Do you think Mummy and Daddy kiss like that?'

'Well, they may do, when they're in bed.'

'Grandad, I feel really sorry for Mummy and Daddy.'

'Sorry? Why?'

''Cos they have to share a bed and I have a bed all to myself. 'Cept I have to share with Basil, but he doesn't take up much room.'

'I think grown-ups like sharing.'

'Do you and Granny share a bed?'

'Yes.'

'Even though you're old?'

'Lucy, I do wish you wouldn't keep going on about my being...'

'Look, Grandad, there's a fairy!'

'Where?'

'Over by the... It's flewed off.'

'Oh well. What was it doing?'

'Just sort of flitting. I 'spect it was a young one, 'cos Miss Nicholls says fairies don't normally show themselves.'

'Are you sure it wasn't a butterfly?'

'Miss Nicholls says that when butterflies die they change into fairies.'

'Your Miss Nicholls sounds very profound.'

'What's profound?'

'It means thinking deep thoughts.'

'Basil's profound. He's always asking me difficult questions 'bout stars and tooth fairies and 'tricity and Father Christmas and...'

'Come on, Lucy, time to feed the ducks.'

'All right. Come on, Basil, we're going to feed the ducks.'

'Not too fast, Lucy.'

The two of them made their way to the edge of the lake.

'Some for you, and some for you. Don't you be so greedy; you've already had some. Here you are, Grandad, you give them some. Careful you don't fall in.'

'You think I might fall in?'

'That's what Mummy always says to me. A big bit for you. 'Cos she gets worried when I get near the edge and she looks after me. Go away; you've had your share. And 'cos Mummy's not here now, I'm sort of looking after you, aren't I, Grandad?'

'That's very kind of you, Lucy.'

'When me and Mummy was here…'

'When Mummy and I were here, Lucy.'

'No, Grandad, it wasn't you and Mummy. It was me and Mummy. You're Mr Greedy; you're not getting anymore. We saw someone fall in and get drownded.'

'That's terrible.'

''Cept she didn't drown, she just pretended. Then she jumped up and shook her hair just like she was a dog and made everyone wet. Here, you two can share that piece. And she thought that was very funny, but no one else thought it was funny.'

'No, I don't suppose they did. That's not at all funny.'

'Like when Harry pretended he was clergy like Darren, and he rolled on the floor and made his face go red and Miss Nicholls sent him to Mrs Anderson.'

'Who's Mrs Anderson?'

'She's our head teacher. There we are, ducks, all finished.'

'What did Mrs Anderson do?'

'I can't remember.'

'Lucy, do you mind if we go and sit down on the bench again?'

'Are you feeling tired, Grandad?'

'Yes. Yes, I am.'

'How tired?'

'Really quite tired.'

'Hold my hand, Grandad, you seem a bit wobbly.'

'Do I?'

'Are you going to be all right, Grandad?'

'I'm… I'm sure I'm going to… to be all right.'

'I'll look after you, Grandad.'

'Thank you, Lucy; I'd like that. I'd like that very much.'

'Me and Basil will look after you.'

The girl was still holding the man's hand when the paramedics arrived.

JESSICA

Carolyn Belcher

Castor oil, bicarbonate of soda and orange juice,
a bilious cocktail in a bath. Why?
Fear of hospital, home birth essential,
I cannot be induced. Aargh!
Crunching pains, a rush of fluid.
Is it diarrhoea or the beginning?
Feels like the end.
The midwife arrives just in time,
so rushed, the gender isn't known.
A boy? A girl? She has to check,
a girl, my daughter.

The bonding, strong in infancy,
suffers fractures in adolescence. Why?
A clash of wills,
like meeting like, head on.
'I want to go to the club, Becky does.'
'No daughter, no. You're only fifteen.'
'I could die tomorrow,
and never have known happiness.'
I laugh, as images from the past
slide into focus;
a similar scene, a repeating pattern,

mother to daughter.

A few years later,
the bond is re-forged.
We're equal now.
My daughter is my friend.
She is bold, and beautiful.
She understands my mistakes.
She is wise, can counsel me,
for she too finds it
hard to be strong,
in the face of male logic.
I recognise that
she has moved further
in thirty-nine years
than I have in sixty-four,
my daughter.

A Traveller's Tale

Russell Kemp

I'd been to Venice that afternoon, for lunch with a client, and taking care to show some old-fashioned respect for his hospitality, hadn't hurried away after the deal had been done. It was late afternoon when I finally made it back to Santa Lucia station, slightly the worse for wear.

The fast intercity train that I'd hoped to catch had just left, and with the next one being in an hour's time, the only alternative was the much slower, more crowded, local train leaving in five minutes. Needing the "john" I visited the station buffet for a sobering shot of coffee as well. By the time I clambered onto the train, the darned thing was practically full, and I had to tramp pretty well the whole length of it to find an empty seat.

I was just settling into one when the door crashed open and two backpackers bundled their way in. Not your usual, disheveled, sweaty nerds mind you, but two of the most glamorous hikers that Italy could ever have seen (but both of them just old enough to have been my mother, I might add). Fighting to stay upright under their massive loads, they made a bee-line for the vacant seats opposite. I wasn't sure who was the soberest, them or me. They staggered about in the confined space, trying to unhitch their packs. Ever the man to assist a lady with removing her things, I offered some help.

'That's quite some load you have there. Would you like a hand?' I said with the bravado gained by my customer's Grappa. (They had American or Canadian written all over them) 'You going mountaineering or something?'

Marcie swept her eyelashes over her incredibly blue eyes and I was lost.

'Why thank you, sir; it sure is, but no, we're going on a cruise tomorrow. We thought we would have one night in Venice first, but can you believe? We've just travelled all the way from the airport to our hotel, and they've double booked!'

'I'm afraid that's quite common in Venice,' I replied, as I placed her load on the floor.

'Really?' said raven-haired Evelyn. 'That's too bad; we booked weeks ago.'

Evelyn's voice was audible chocolate, and infused with the rich New England burr that is so attractive in mature American ladies. I was quite taken by this cosmopolitan duo and enjoyed their different style of conversation. They complemented each other, opposites yet so alike. I'm still not sure which one I preferred, Marcie, a bubbly, platinum-blonde Madonna look-alike, or Evelyn, slightly more reserved, more thoughtful.

'The hotel receptionists were so helpful,' Marcie continued. 'They phoned all around for us, but there are no rooms available in Venice itself tonight.'

'Now we have to go back to Mestre, to a sister hotel,' said Evelyn,—'the Royale, near the station.'

'Don't go there,' I blurted out. 'That's an awful place to stay— dirty, noisy and a rip-off joint for foreign tourists! Why don't you come and stay at my family's hotel, located in beautiful countryside near Mestre. We think it's the best small hotel outside of Venice. I'm sure my Aunt will make you welcome.'

My new friends seemed quite touched.

'Well that's very kind of you, if you're sure your Aunt has vacancies. What do you think Evelyn?'

'Sure, sounds OK to me. I hope you don't mind me saying, but you speak very good English!'

'That's because I am English, though of Italian descent. Let me introduce myself, I'm Umberto Price from Bedford, England.'

'Umberto! Well how do you do? Has anybody ever told you, you look just like Leonardo DiCaprio?'

The Hotel Mulinaccio stands impressively amid shady gardens and terraces at the end of a long, straight Roman road. As though losing its nerve before it encroaches upon the building's domain, the road deviates sharply and continues on its way to Padova. The gravel drive splays out amongst the topiary, a welcoming hand, guiding visitors through the garden to the pink-arched foyer. The thick stone walls have stood from at least the fifteenth century, and have witnessed the lives of all the generations of my family from that time.

Why the place is not called the Hotel Speroni I can't say (apart from my family's hate of breaking traditions). I use the term "family" lightly, as I am not a true Speroni. My Father breezed in for a couple of nights in 1978 and Mamma was overwhelmed by his razzmatazz. Conceived on site, I was born in England nine months later. Although Mamma has spent most of her married life in England, she has dutifully maintained daily contact with her family in Veneto, where blood relations are as important as Valpolicella. So we've always returned there. Having the advantage of being bilingual and of the family connection in the locality, I found much tourist-related business in the area. That said, it was implicit that I returned whenever possible.

We drove from Mestre station to the Mulinaccio in my car, I was enormously proud to take my new friends home, and as we got out, the evening chimes of the bells of San Benedetto floated across the fields from the village.

It was Evelyn who reacted first. 'Oh my, how quaint! Even

the church bells play chintzy little tunes.'

'I could eat this place. It's fairytale, pure Disney!' gushed Marcie.

I'm not sure what my family would have thought to this, and I couldn't bring myself to tell Evelyn the campanology was a deception worthy of Hollywood.

'Just wait till you see inside,' I replied instead.

Aunt Violette was not so enthusiastic when I introduced my two companions. I`d forgotten the school trip of thirty sixth-formers, staying that night.

'Where do you expect them to sleep then?' she asked suspiciously in Italian.

'I think they are a bit too old for me, Violette.' I said.

Mindful of family honour and my fiancée Francesca back home in England, she clearly didn`t think so.

'Hm!'

'They can have my room,' I said. 'I'll sleep on the fold-down put-you-up in the office.'

Violette approved of Fran. Fran was Front-of-House in her father's restaurant (Italian, of course) in Brighton. Her family had connections in Veneto too. Violette's great hope was that when we eventually married, we would buy out her share of the business and take over the running of the Mulinaccio.

We were having our dinner out in the warm evening air of the terrace when the students appeared. Those who were not already an item, were weighing each other up. It was a bit of a cattle market. Lots of flashing eyes and exaggerated pelvis wriggling from the girls, and cool, indifferent, posturing from the boys. I found this all a bit tacky, but who was I to criticise them when I wanted to achieve the same result myself? We lingered at the table in the true Italian tradition, chatting to other guests, and sipping lemon liqueur. The kids gobbled their pizzas and were gone. The Mulinaccio pulsated noisy, exuberant life. Music played, lights shone out of every window, everybody was happy, amore was in the air and it was affecting me.

Violette and her staff were rushed off their feet. I felt guilty about not helping, but I was now intoxicated by my guests. My ego rose as they treated me like some demi-god, hanging on my every word. Later, I led them through the grounds and down to the stream. Fish were rising, frogs were croaking, and something was going on behind the bushes that was not on the syllabus. I felt quite ignorant and unsophisticated, when they spoke of the similarities of Veneto and New England, the climate in summer, the fast train between Boston and New York, and the Universities in Providence where they both worked. Most of all I was envious of their freedom, of how at the end of each semester they would pack their bags and travel pretty much wherever they chose. I loved their company, but what could I do when I didn't even know which one of them I liked the best? How many young men would have had the confidence to attempt the simultaneous pleasuring of two older signoras? There again, was I reading too much into the situation? At around midnight I wished them Buona Notte and headed for the office. They seemed disappointed, perhaps they'd hoped for more, but a threesome was out of the question. I had to be up early in the morning and Violette would have been watching. I wished that they were not leaving so soon, but I consoled myself with the fact that at least I would be taking them back to the station on my way to Milan.

The office sofa was not a very comfortable billet and I dozed fitfully; the sounds of numerous nocturnal visits happening upstairs didn't help. Around two o'clock, the door opened with a creak. I raised an eyelid hopefully, only to see the face of my Aunt peering at me through the half-light. Whoever got lucky that night, it was not going to be me.

She was much happier the next morning when the "girls"

checked out and we left for the station. I was almost glad that we were still Virgo Intacta so to speak, when we parted at the ticket office. There were no regrets or embarrassments; with hugs and kisses we said our goodbyes. Our trains travelled in opposite directions, and were leaving at much the same time from different platforms, mine to Milan being quite a way off. I tried to think about the report of the previous day's business that I had to write during my journey as I wandered down the underpass, but I couldn't get the women out of my mind. At that moment it all seemed such a waste of my life, a young guy like me carrying all this responsibility, when I ought to be travelling the world enjoying what it had to offer. In a flash it came upon me.

'Bugger Milan,' I said to myself. I turned around and hurried back through the tunnel. I would travel with Marcie and Evelyn to Venice and book a berth on their ship. We would travel together around the Adriatic then on to who knows where?

I searched impatiently along the crowded Venice platform, aching to surprise them with my reappearance and momentous change-of-life plan.

The train pulled in, and as the doors opened I saw them walking unencumbered across the platform. Carrying their luggage were two young Adonises, their tongues nearly dragging on the floor as the pair led on their latest pieces of arm-candy. Anger flared inside me as I realised what a fool I'd been and how I'd been used.

'Bloody Yankee hustlers,' I gasped, hurting as though just shot by a gun. Some women nearby heard, but I didn't care. I moved behind a group of people and stood, eyes watering while I looked on wretchedly, acting like a peeping-tom as the train filled, then transported them out of my life.

When it was gone, a voice inside me said: 'You tosser! That's the way it is. Get over it. Get on with your own life.'

So I sat down on a seat, and got out my mobile-phone to text Fran. I wrote, 'Dear Fran, There's no nice way to say this. I don't want to marry you anymore. It's over. We're finished. We're through.'

Then I walked into town and bought a rucksack.

The Utah Gun Prison & Pizza Company

Nigel George

R on James stood outside the Holiday Inn. He looked at the
screwed up piece of paper he'd taken from his pocket.

Interview: 9.30 a.m.
Harvey J Wiengold III
Utah Gun Prison & Pizza Company

Ron couldn't fathom what he was doing at a hotel if it was an
interview for a job as a prison guard. He reached into his other
pocket and removed the remains of a pork pie. Oblivious to
the parking sticker attached to it, he rammed the pie into his
mouth, as his eyes flicked from the paper to the hotel sign.
The reassuring taste of pastry and pork fat calmed Ron's
nerves. He walked into the hotel's reception. Why someone
who suffered from claustrophobia would want to be a prison
guard would have been a mystery to most. Ron however had
found the cure: as long as he had a pie to eat, he could keep
his fears at bay.

'I'm here to see Mr Wiengold,' he said with a broad greasy
smile.

'Down the corridor, third door on the left,' said the
receptionist.

'Thank you.' As Ron walked away from the desk, he turned

and went back.

'You don't sell pies, do you?'

The receptionist gave him a quizzical look. 'Pies?'

'Yes. Pork pies, chicken and mushroom, steak and kidney, or a nice pasty if you have it,' said Ron with growing enthusiasm.'

'We've got salmon en croute on our lunchtime Busy Traveller menu.'

'No, I'm after a pie, not a croute.'

'The salmon en croute comes in pastry.'

'I'll take three, please!'

'They're only available in our Voyager restaurant. We don't start serving lunch for three hours.'

'Oh.' Deflated, Ron walked down the corridor and was ushered in to see Harvey Wiengold.

A large American came from behind a desk and shook his hand with a warm smile, as if Ron were a long-lost friend. He beckoned him to a chair and sat down behind the desk.

'Mr James, my name is Harvey J. Wiengold. Welcome to the Utah Gun Prison & Pizza Company.'

'I like your pizzas.'

'I'm very pleased to hear that.'

'Have you thought of doing one with a pork pie topping?'

'Excuse me?'

'You know, pork pies.' Ron could see the look of bemusement on Weingold's face and decided to change the subject. 'I picked up one of your job applications in the local pizza place. They said it was closing down.'

'Yes, unfortunately the business model doesn't work for us in this country, we aren't allowed to use the same marketing slogan we use back home: "Feed and defend your family."'

'Defend?'

'Yes in the States you get a free gun with every pizza. We tried it with knives in this country but it wasn't the same, and your Government objected anyway. You see, Mr James, guns, prisons and pizza are the perfect combination. Pizza is the ideal food to feed prisoners on. It's cheap to make and it's far harder for fat prisoners to escape. Although we have the occasional problem with prisoners who get so fat we can't get them out of their cells.'

'What about the guns?'

Weingold spread his hands and gave Ron a broad smile. 'Everybody needs a gun.'

Ron James nodded. His eyes took in the nameplate in front of Wiengold that announced him to be Harvey J. Wiengold III.

'I had a Mark III Cortina once,' said Ron. He always thought a joke at an interview was a good idea.

'Excuse me?'

'Your name, Harvey Wiengold Mark III. That makes you the latest model does it?' added Ron, having no idea when to stop.

The American blinked. He'd been in the UK for 24 hours and it was his first visit. Perhaps this was how all Brits acted.

'No, Mr James, I'm just Harvey J. Wiengold the *third*. Named after my father and grandfather.'

Ron nodded enthusiastically.

'Mr James. It says on your application form that your last job was as a traffic warden. We don't have traffic wardens in the States, but we do have prison wardens, which is a pretty responsible job. He's the guy who's in charge of the whole prison.'

'Yeah, that's right,' said Ron, catching on quickly to the American's wholly unexpected line of thinking. 'I was in charge of all the traffic…prison section.'

The American looked at him quizzically.

'We don't mess around in this country, anyone caught speeding and we lock them up, no messing. I was in charge of all of that.'

The American beamed and stretched out his hand.

'Welcome to the Utah Gun Prison & Pizza Company. You're just the kind of man we need.'

Ron James drove his aged car through the main gates of the East Cheam holding centre of the Utah Gun Prison & Pizza Company. The ten-foot high fence, topped with razor wire and CCTV cameras, spoke of a high security area. For anyone in doubt a large sign pronounced:

THIS IS A HIGH SECURITY AREA
AUTHORISED PERSONNEL ONLY

He parked his car and passed through the large double doors leading to reception. As Ron entered, he was greeted by a cardboard cut-out of a nubile young woman dressed in thong, fur boots and Russian hat. She was clutching a machine gun and her naked breasts were concealed behind two pizzas which bore the logo KALASHNIKOVA PIZZA.

He stood transfixed. Slowly he took the remains of a pork pie from his pocket and absentmindedly put it into his mouth, his reverie only broken as the pie slipped down his throat.

Looking around, he saw the reception desk and walked towards it. Two young women sat behind it deep in conversation about the latest developments in a late-night soap opera, which one had seen and the other missed.

'So she took him home, right…'

'Not that Darren?'

'Yeah and…' the girl rolled her eyes in annoyance as the phone softly purred. She pushed a button on the console in front of her and spoke into her headset. 'Utah Gun Prison & Pizza Company, how can I help you? You want to make a complaint about a death in custody? One moment please.' She put the call on hold. 'Yeah, that Darren.'

'He's got his top off in this magazine.'

'Ooh! Let's have a look.' The two women ogled the pictures of Darren's digitally enhanced chest. The phone purred again.

The girl pushed the button on the console. 'Sorry, what was it you were calling about? Your dead uncle? One moment.' She put the call back on hold and turned to the other girl.

'He says he wants to know what we're doing about his dead uncle.'

'He needs to speak to Barry if it's a death in custody, but he's on holiday this week.'

'Oh yeah.' The receptionist pushed the button again. 'Hello, you need to speak to Barry Swallow, but he's on holiday this week. It's urgent? You did say your uncle was dead? Well it can't be that urgent then can it?' A puzzled frown came over her face. She turned to the other receptionist. 'He hung up! No pleasing some people.'

The two women finally noticed Ron standing at the reception desk.

'Hello, can I help?' asked the girl.

'Mr Wiengold sent me.'

The other receptionist looked at Ron and giggled. 'You look just like Fat Trevor off the telly.'

'Oh yeah,' said the girl.

Ron smiled. 'I was told to report to a Phil Stubbins.'

'He's through in the lock-up, but you need a pass to go down there. Have you got one?'

Ron shook his head.

'Can't let you down there without a pass,' said the other receptionist.

'Oh look,' said the girl. 'Here's one, we can use this, what's your name?'

'Ron James.'

She looked at the pass. It showed a swarthy face and bore the name Zoltan Zygbinev.

'Well if you want to go down the lock-up today, you're going to have to be Zoltan Zygbinev.'

'But he don't look nothing like Zoltan. Zoltan was dark, all over!' added the other receptionist with a giggle.'

'You got a photo?' asked the girl.

Ron shook his head.

'I tell you what,' said the other receptionist. 'There's a picture of Fat Trevor in my magazine—we can use that.'

Ten minutes later Ron James, aka Zoltan Zygbinev, walked into the lock-up. The picture of Fat Trevor was remarkably similar to that of Ron. Fat Trevor was drunk in the picture and had a face that resembled a pig's head after someone had repeatedly slammed a door shut on it. The resemblance to Ron was uncanny. As it turned out, the hard work of the two girls went unrewarded. The gate to the lock-up was propped open with a fire extinguisher; Ron walked right in.

In the main holding area, Phil Stubbins and Tony Lockwood were trying to inject one of their prisoners with a horse tranquiliser known as ketamine. They didn't know it was used to knock out horses. They'd only been told it was a sedative for prisoners who might prove troublesome during transport. As guards were expected to transport prisoners in their own cars alone, they had no hesitation in giving it to anyone who so much as coughed when he shouldn't. James "Tiger" McGivens had been through their hands several times, and there was no doubt he would cause trouble given half a chance. Lockwood had spent half an hour looking for a bigger syringe so they could inject an extra large dose of the ketamine into him. He had discussed with Stubbins whether he should go home and borrow his wife's icing gun but had been dissuaded when Stubbins pointed out that they would never get the needle to fit in the end and the average icing gun wasn't sharp enough to pierce human skin.

Although Tiger McGivens was quite partial to the out-of-body experience you got when taking ketamine, he objected on a point of principle to having screws sedate him. Although no legal genius, even the few remaining amphetamine-soaked brain cells in his head told him that there was something illegal in what was going on. More to the point, he was scared of needles.

'You're not sticking that in me!' he said.

'Come on, Tiger, don't misbehave,' said Lockwood.

As Ron walked into the holding area he saw Stubbins approach Tiger from behind with a baseball bat while Lockwood distracted him with the needle. The first blow from the bat struck Tiger's head. He looked bewildered and rubbed the top as if he'd felt rain. Ron looked on in bemusement as the next blow to Tiger's kidneys sent him crashing to his knees. Lockwood now picked up a pickaxe handle and the two men rained blows down until he fell unconscious to the floor.

Having finished their assault on Tiger the two men noticed Ron.

'Who are you?' asked Stubbins.

'Ron James. I'm looking for Mr Stubbins. But I can see you're busy. I'll come back later.'

Ron turned and tried to walk casually from the room, as if he'd witnessed no more than some mild embarrassment.

'Hang on a minute,' said Stubbins.

Ron turned, a nervous smile on his lips. He drew an imaginary zip across his mouth.

The light came on in Stubbins head. 'Oh! No need to worry about that. You the new bloke head office have sent?'

Ron nodded.

'Good, we've been a bit shorthanded. Cup of tea?'

Ron nodded again, keeping half an eye on the door.

'Have you killed him?' he whispered.

'Nah,' said Lockwood dunking a biscuit in the cup of tea he'd picked up, 'don't think so. He's not dead is he Phil?' He turned to Stubbins.

'Nah, don't think so,' replied Stubbins, 'I've checked; he's still breathing.'

The three men looked at Tiger. No one fancied getting too close to him. Even lying unconscious on the floor, Tiger was still pretty scary.

'You want a biscuit with your tea?' Stubbins asked Ron.

The three men sat in quiet contemplation, sipping their tea and dunking biscuits.

'We like to call this our quiet time,' said Lockwood. 'You need a few minutes to chill out when you've had to confront a stubborn prisoner.'

Ron nodded. He felt more secure with the warm tea and munched on his fifth biscuit. 'How do you know he'll be all right?' he asked.

'It's not the first time we've had to tell Tiger to be quiet, is it Phil?' said Lockwood.

Stubbins nodded and then added. 'We done it lots of times. It don't hurt him. He's a tough old bastard.'

'Don't like needles though,' mumbled Lockwood through a mouthful of biscuit. Stubbins nodded in agreement.

'What were you trying to inject him with?' asked Ron.

'A needle,' said Lockwood ramming another biscuit into his mouth.

'Oh,' said Ron. The three men drank tea, their reverie only broken by a groaning sound from the floor.

'Bugger,' said Lockwood. 'We better hurry up and give him the jab.' He turned to Ron. 'Pass me that syringe, mate.'

'What's in it?' asked Ron as he handed it over.

Lockwood looked to Stubbins for guidance. Stubbins took the syringe from him and peered at it in the hope it would help. The name of the German manufacturer was printed on the side, but Stubbins was fairly sure the contents were called something different. However, he was in charge of the injection, having done a St John Ambulance course, and didn't want to appear ignorant. 'We're giving him a Muller,' he said.

'A Muller?' queried Ron. 'What does a Muller do?'

'Makes 'em sleepy,' butted in Lockwood, keen to show that Stubbins wasn't the sole fount of medical knowledge.

'Sleepy? What for?'

'You got to sedate them before you put them in the car. Company policy,' said Stubbins. Lockwood nodded vigorously in support.

'Car? Don't you have a van for transporting prisoners?'

'No. Head Office say that using a van is bad for the environment.'

'Yeah! We've got to watch our carbon whatsits,' added Lockwood.

'He means footprint, got to watch our carbon footprint, so we try and deliver prisoners in our cars on the way home. But you got to sedate them if you think they might get a bit frisky.'

'That's health and safety,' said Lockwood.

'How do you decide who'll get frisky?' asked Ron.

'Well, if they object to being jabbed with a needle I suppose,' replied Stubbins.

'What happens if you don't have a car?'

'We did have one bloke who tried taking them on the bus, but you can get some heavy buggers, especially if we've had them a while and they've had too much pizza.'

'It's a right bugger trying to get a sedated prisoner off a bus,' added Lockwood.

'Jerry had a moped.' Stubbins offered.

'Yeah,' said Lockwood. 'That didn't work neither. Prisoners kept falling off the back of it. Difficult to hang on when you're sleeping.'

Another groan came from the floor.

'Come on,' said Stubbins, 'let's find a vein and get him sorted.'

'What's a vein?' asked Lockwood, as he stabbed the needle casually into Tiger's arm.

BLUEWATER

Wilf Jones

In the quarry
Strange doings:
The fallen laboured night and day
With the hard machinery of commerce
For the sake of future gain.

The noise they made,
The ruin,
The pan-demonic din of pain
Echoed loud, redoubled and
Called to the reeling sky:

"Witness this creation!
See what we have made:
A palace built of open pride,
Come see how we have prayed.
This lofty temple is un-fathered,
A theatre of delight;
We open doors to everyone,
Bring all to see the light."

And the voice called out unchallenged,
Climbed all the way to the stars,

And further it flew, still further
While the faithful parked their cars.

And all there dared to believe
It was not so bad to hear
No reply.

REALITY

Wilf Jones

Two great ships
Dominate this reach of London's flow,
Never moving:
Stranded on an Island
That is not an island.

They are connected to the low cloud
By smoke-stacks so tall
These vessels would turn turtle
Released from moorings.

From a break-line in the grey canopy
Failing light draws down
Making of these hulks grim
Shadows of cold power.

Do they soak up and transform the energy,
Extracting the life
From the sands they straddle?

Lesser trade surge beneath,
Their thousands of tons
Reduced to scale on the water.

How small then are the oystercatchers of men
Foraging this Essex fore-shore?
Fourteen at a glance, bent double,
Connected to the mud by silhouettes of shovels.
Is it only oysters they treasure,
Or scallops, or kelp or any of these,
Or the daily small-time endeavour
That pretends to make them more real?

Powering the city
The turbines drone unheard,
Undisturbed at this distance
By the caddis-fly scavengers
Of this oft-drained shore,
Knowing of purpose,
Safe in function.

Dancing

Wilf Jones

The pebble beach invades
          the promenade.
Look:
Landside cast in piles of stone
     make detour
     for shoes and paws,
     balletic blades, all skip and spin;
At
Seaside sand so rarely seen
     for all those cast off
     souls so hard
     is bare;
And
In between great mounds thrown up
     by wanton movement,
     sea and air,
     echo the rising Down.

With a broom could we push back tide
     clearing pavement, clearing time?

Till then
We sprites of waves all pirouette

in space between vast energies,

We dance above the shoreline,
    beyond the shingle lip and lap,
We dance before the next great storm
    rides in to pound our lives.

Surprise Treasures

Eleanor Castleden

ook at that gorgeous baby. Isn't he sweet?' said Audrey
to her friend, Margaret. 'Don't you just love his little blue
outfit?'

'Do you think that's his mum or his granny?' said Margaret.

'Probably his granny, although there are older mums and
dads nowadays,' said Audrey.

The baby's mother was holding him proudly in front of her
and stroking his fair hair.

Audrey and Margaret were enjoying their weekly day out:
a browse round the antiques centre in the morning, followed
by lunch in the local coffee shop. They'd been friends since
both their husbands had died, and looked forward to their
Wednesdays together. They both dabbled in antiques, and
what had started as a hobby had turned into a way of earning
a few pennies; enough for their lunches out and presents for
their grandchildren.

'Yes he's a real cutie, isn't he? He reminds me of my little
grandson, James. Enjoy him while you can,' she said to the
woman. 'They grow up so quickly. What's his name?'

'Harry,' said the woman.

'How old is he?' asked Margaret.

'Almost five months. We're looking for an antique rocking
chair for him.'

'I've found one.' A man appeared. Presumably he was the woman's husband.

The woman looked delighted. 'Perfect,' she said. 'They only want thirty pounds for it. Let's offer twenty five and see what they say, Jack. I'll just pop Harry into it, to see if it fits him.'

'He's a very well-behaved baby, isn't he?' Audrey whispered to Margaret.

'And quiet.'

The man must have overheard them for he said, 'They're all like this. No fuss or bother at all.'

'All?' Audrey and Margaret spoke together.

'We've five more at home, two girls and two boys. They're asleep in their car-seats in the lounge. It's Amanda's turn to be taken out tomorrow.'

'I've just seen a Bunnikins mug,' said the woman. 'Let's get that as well. I think we ought to pay now, Jack. It's getting near Harry's feed. We can go to the coffee shop. It's your turn to change him, don't forget.'

'Could I hold him before you go?' said Audrey.

'Of course,' the woman handed Harry to Audrey.

'Oh!' she said.

The woman smiled. 'You thought he was real, didn't you?'

'Yes. I mean his little face is all screwed up, just like a new-born baby. He's…' She didn't know what to say.

'We bought him from a site on the internet. We've bought all of them that way. Our children have grown up and left home and…well our new family have filled the gap. These babies are much easier to look after. We wash and change them twice a day. They wake up when we wake up. And like I said before, we give them turns in going out with us.'

'Do they all look the same?' asked Audrey.

'Oh no, we have dark-haired children as well as fair. They have human hair, you know. The detail's marvellous. If we'd wanted, we could have sent photos of our children as babies and an artist would have copied their features. But that would have cost a lot more than the four hundred pounds we paid. Ah, here's Jack. Well it's been nice meeting you two ladies, bye-bye.'

'Well!' said Audrey. 'I don't know about you, Margaret, but that's put me right off hunting for Wedgewood blue and white china.'

'I totally agree. I think it's time for lunch, and I'm going to have an extra-large piece of carrot cake with a cuppa for dessert.'

'What a good idea! Vinyl babies indeed! What are you laughing about?'

'I was just thinking that there might be a site where they offered vinyl husbands. That would be good, wouldn't it? No talking about football, no arguing; we'd always be right and we could choose what to watch on the telly.'

'Plus they'd be light enough to haul up the stairs at night. They wouldn't make saucy demands, and more importantly, they wouldn't snore.'

'I think we've got a really good idea there, Audrey; no socks or pants on the floor, no wet towels on the tiles.'

'No tools left lying about for us to trip over.'

'Shall we go round to library after lunch and see what the internet throws up? You never know what we might find...'

PUNISHING THE INNOCENT

Julian Corbell

You so much liked climbing trees and running on the Doctor's big lawn. And most of all, you loved playing on that car that was really only a tree-stump. You never had to think of what to wear or where your mother was. You didn't know there were any problems in life; you just went from one play-day to another. If the sun shone you were outside, running about, climbing, hiding, shouting, laughing, right until the sun went down. Then you just went into the little cottage, had some food, made some plasticine models, and then slept—with perhaps a bit of a pillow-fight with your brother. Do you suppose that was Heaven and this is Hell?

This is what is called Boarding School and you are not at all sure how or why you are here. Every day you have to wear a proper shirt, trousers and shoes and have to wait to go outside. You sit in dreary classrooms longer than you want, with boys you don't like, and teachers who don't seem to like you. There are only two bits of fun: writing stories in the afternoon, and playing on the field until bedtime, which is too early. You don't like sleeping in a big dormitory with eleven other boys, and you certainly don't like being bathed and having your hair washed by a strange woman. You just hate what some of the boys make you do, things you don't understand but which seem to make them all laugh. And even if you don't make any noise in the dorm, you get punished as if you had, six whacks of a slipper on your bum while wearing only pyjamas. And you don't know where you are or when you'll get home again.

You used to like running barefoot, thought it was fun. Now you have to put on special boots that hurt, stand in special positions on a big field and get kicked by other boys who seem to enjoy it. You thought football was just fun, kicking a ball when you wanted to, or leaving it when you didn't. Now you get shouted at when you miss it. And there's a new game that you really don't like, with an odd-shaped ball that doesn't bounce the way a ball should. You wanted to hold it and get used to it, but as soon as you did a bigger boy grabbed you in a very rough fashion and threw you to the ground. And laughed. Don't you just hate it? If this isn't Hell, you sure don't want to find out what is.

On Saturday mornings you have to sit in a class-room with a teacher to write a letter home. Though you didn't know it, this was your introduction to Public Relations. You were given special writing paper, with the lines ruled in threes, one broad and two narrow, so that your small letters fitted into the narrow lines and your capitals reached up to the wide one. Your first letter home was usually rejected, on the grounds that it was saying too much or was too emotional—you have just been introduced to Censorship. If you were intelligent, and you soon discovered that you were, you quickly noticed that dutiful letters about good school experiences would pass. In fact, if you did this several weeks running, the teacher would eventually accept that your letter was good enough not to need seeing before it was sent. That was the moment that you wrote the truth. Your truth was that you were very unhappy and felt like crying much of the time and wanted to leave this school. That was the moment that you also drew a little picture of yourself at the end, looking very sad and in tears, which dropped from your eyes and collected in a pool at the bottom of the page. You tried not to smile at all as the envelope was sealed and the letter was sent, but you did look forward to your mother's reply.

Sunday is your worst day of all. Whatever the morning is like, and however good the midday meal, you know that you will be forced out for a long walk in the afternoon. You'll have to walk in twos, in what they call a "crocodile", all the way through the town where you get pointed at, then all the way round the countryside, past the Squinting Cat Public House, up endless winding lanes, stopping only to hear some mysterious jokes by the Prefects who are in charge of you. Your feet hurt, you can't rest when you feel tired, and you have to walk behind boys who talk about you as if you don't belong. Worse still, you have to write about it when you get back, in a way that makes it sound as if it was fun. That may have been your introduction to what is called Fiction, but to you it sounds like Lies.

The worst part of Sunday is saved until last. It is called Chapel. After dinner, all the boys and all the Masters proceed into the school chapel for the evening service. There is much talk of God and Love, but these two desirable items seem to be completely absent. No-one smiles at you or makes you welcome. If the day did dawn bright and clear, by the end of it you have almost forgotten who you are. Your school number is 361, which you know well, as it is sewn into everything you wear. Your elder brother doesn't speak to you, being in a much higher class, your mother only visits once a term, and your father doesn't see you at all. Occasionally you hear of a strange place called Character Building but don't ever see it.

There is supposed to be a bright spot in each week, called Tuck Shop. There is no real shop, only a collection of tuck-boxes, each one supplied by your parents and kept in a special locked room. Every Friday you are allowed to go to this room, open your own tuck-box and choose yourself a special treat. Some of the tuck-boxes are hand-made, some are obviously bought from very expensive shops, and most of them are huge. Yours is a small brown case, just big enough to contain a few half-size tins and jars. Your special treat is a tin of blackcurrant purée, much laughed at and looked down on by your form-mates with bigger boxes. Not once does anyone think to offer you something better from their box. Later you learn that this is called OneUpManShip, and is very important to success in Life.

Consequences

Russell Kemp

'It was just a thought,' he said.
Rekindled dreams of long ago,
Received, rebuffed, rescinded.
Unwanted, aging, Lothario.
Whose claims of love do not impress,
The lady who would know.

Feckless, wet-lipped, youth club kisses,
Given freely by the score.
But mere kisses were not enough,
He wanted so much more.
Unfaithful, betrayed her hippy beads and tresses;
Lust found another paramour.

Sweethearts once, but torn apart,
By the reproductive madness,
That burns a man within.
One indiscretion and a lifetime of regret;
Her children are not his.
Bitter rewards of sin.

FLIGHTS OF FANCY

Pat Christie

'The mummers are here! The mummers are here!' The shout resounded through the market place. A young boy, on his way to school, quickly turned round and followed the crowd to the green where a travelling fair had been set up.

'This is too good to be missed,' he said to himself. 'I don't care if it means a beating when I get to school.' He sat cross-legged on the ground in front of the stage and watched in wonder at the performance. How he longed to join the actors in their flights of fancy to other lands, to other ages—a battle here, a court scene there, a storm at sea. He marvelled at the antics of the comedians and was entranced by it all.

The church clock tolled the twelfth hour and he reluctantly left the green, pausing briefly to look at the fire-eater, the dancing bear, the cock fight and all the other attractions of the fair. By the time he got to school the scholars had reassembled after the break and his absence earned him a beating and a detention at the end of the school day.

On his way home he went down to the river, a favourite spot for his musings. Idly he threw sticks in the water and watched their progress. If only he had a boat and could travel to foreign lands. Perhaps he'd meet pirates on the way. Or else he'd be a brave sailor fighting for his country and good Queen Bess. Maybe he'd land on a desert island and wrestle with the natives, travel back in time to ancient Rome and be a gladiator, discover new countries with exotic beasts.

With a sigh he got up and wandered his way through the town. Passing an inn with sounds of bawdy laughter coming forth was too much for his curiosity and he crept in under one of the tables.

'Wench! Bring us more ale,' shouted one of the men. A buxom female approached and the boy's eyes nearly started out of his head at the sight of her plump boobies.

'Ripe pomegranates, these,' shouted a drunken oaf as he made a grab for her. She boxed his ears and then glanced under the table.

'You young scamp!' she exclaimed. 'Git out of 'ere,' and with a sharp kick she propelled him into the street.

By the time he got home it was late. His mother shook her fist at him.

'Look at the state of your breeches,' she shrieked. 'Bed for you, my lad, and no supper.'

The next morning he took his usual route through the woods —imagining warlocks and witches behind every tree, wild beasts and hobgoblins round every bend in the path. Another beating awaited his late arrival at school. He was made to sit in the corner and transcribe vast tracts from the Bible. The schoolmaster remonstrated with him.

'If you don't attend to your lessons, Will Shakespeare. You'll never get anywhere.'

VIENNA

Carolyn Belcher

There is a cold that penetrates so deep inside me, the only way I can get warm is to have a bath. I have been cold since...Dagmar.

Photos of the woman I failed to help are strewn all over the studio floor. I doubt I will ever finish the painting. How can I? Each photo accuses me.

The day that forced me to leave Vienna, never to return, was one of those icing, crisp days. When Dagmar arrived at the studio, for the session I had arranged on the pretext I needed more profile photos, she did not take off her coat.

'I can't stop,' she said. 'I have to go somewhere. I want you to do something for me. I want you to meet me outside the Friedshofskirche at six o'clock precisely. I can't go into the church alone, it's dangerous for me. We can come back here when I've finished what I have to do and....'

She did not complete her sentence, nor did she explain, leaving me stranded with questions, hope, desire, despair. Why would she want me? I am no Midge Ure, mystic and soulful, staring out of the screen; everything about me is ordinary. I am Mr Average. That I am a reasonably successful artist has its attractions, I suppose, but surely not enough to tempt this Viennese beauty into my bed. No, it would be payment for the favour.

When she left the studio, I went to the window to watch her walk down the street. I made a bargain with myself; if she looked up, I would go. If she did not, I would leave her to her fate. Just as the tram came into view, she looked up. She saw me watching. She waved. She smiled. Hooked, I was forced to run with the barb in my mouth, such is slavering lust.

I am not a great timekeeper. I am often late for appointments. My agent is forever telling me off. This day, I had to make sure. 'Six o'clock, precisely,' Dagmar had said. I left the house in plenty of time, and as I walked to the tram stop, I saw my breath floating ahead of me leading the way; leading me into… I stomped up and down on the pavement, trying to keep warm, trying to stop my imagination racing ahead. When the tram arrived, I hesitated. I didn't know Dagmar. Why had I agreed to this folly? It was the picture of her pale beauty, sprawling naked on my bed which spurred me on, and into a seat. I sighed. My breath froze on the windowpane.

'Three stops,' she had said. 'You get off at the third stop. Can you remember that?'

'It isn't difficult to remember,' I had replied.

She had looked at me as though she weren't sure, as though perhaps she needed to say more to fix my promise, but in the end, all she said was, 'Don't be late.'

The Friedshofskirche reminds me of the Sacré-Coeur; it is so white, and winter cold. They are both great edifices to a powerful god whose law is fixed in stone. White, as a colour, consists of many hues. Even though I am conversant with light and pigment I still find that odd. But colours mixed on a palette evolve into an uninviting, sludgy purple, brown, the colour of dried blood. When I had advertised for a model, I had stipulated that I needed someone who would reflect the hues of white. I chose Dagmar. Now she had chosen me.

As I approached the entrance, I heard her voice reaching out to me, through the doors of the church.

'It's too late. You promised and you're too late.'

I looked at my watch. I was on time. Why was she accusing me? To make sure, I got my mobile phone out of my pocket. I willed it to show six. Six-o-one, I could not deny the six-o-one. A minute, surely one minute couldn't have…it was that minute, that damned real-time minute that has chilled my blood and sent me scampering to fill bathtubs with scalding hot water ever since. I froze like the window breath on the tram, as another sound, one that would stay with me until all feeling had gone, assailed my ears. I was a Hamlet, powerless to act, and forever mouthing, "Oh that this too, too solid flesh…".

The sound grew, and soon I was howling with it. I put my hands over my ears to stop the noise, but it was inside me; there was no escape. When it died down, I was crunched in a ball in the doorway. I tried to propel myself forward into the ice church to see what had become of Dagmar, the woman I had hoped to seduce, to paint, to make love to over and over and…but my body refused to uncurl.

I would never kiss her pale lips, stroke her ash blonde hair, gently remove her clothes, and then, trembling, flick my tongue over each nipple, tweak, pinch, until she begged me to enter her. Ah…the music we would have been been playing would grow and grow to…nothing. I was impotent.

Alone, outside a church, I would always be alone, fleeing from hotel to hotel, night after night waiting for daylight to come with its cool, empty silence. I would never feel the warmth of her hand, only the snow falling from a cold, grey sky, as she faded to a distance I could not reach. The fantasy flew through the church doors, and with it the magic of the city. I had to go, to leave Vienna, knowing I could not return. I was a coward.

There is a cold that penetrates so deep inside me that I can never be warm. The name of the cold is, Vienna.

THE NIGHTJAR

Laura Haines

Endless
Whirring song
Vibrating in the still
Dark night. Hidden in the grass;
A thrill.

Churring
A silent flight,
Then with whiskery beaks
Open their ventriloquist's mouth
To speak.

Six O'Clock

Rose O'Meara

To be honest, I'm not very fond of my own company.

There, I've said it out loud. I'm not very fond of my own company. I'll be a little more forthright—I don't like myself or my company, not at all. Now I've said it out loud and been truly honest with myself for once, a devastating feeling has overwhelmed me. It's as if I am standing on the dry ground below a great high dam which has burst and a towering wall of water is rushing towards me. All my past life, the broken promises, the lies, the endless lies, are threatening to engulf me. I don't like my own company. Full stop. I don't like my own company. The last few years have been a sham, a pretence of such great magnitude that I'm astounded at my own duplicity. What am I going to do now? Why, oh why didn't I listen to that horrible, niggling little voice, that tiny but insistent voice in my mind which kept saying "Don't do it, don't do it" and which wriggled its way into my consciousness whenever my stern concentration was wavering? What did I think was going to happen?

Tonight at six o'clock Sister Mathilda will be coming to collect me from my cell to take me before all the Sisters and Mother Superior in the chapel, and there will be a night of prayers and intercessions. I will be wearing my short postulant's habit for the last time. Tomorrow there will be a well-rehearsed ceremony and I will cease to be Susan Ellis, misfit extraordinaire, self-harmer, and alcoholic. I will become Sister Mary-Frances, a nun in the contemplative order of St Joseph, vowed to poverty, chastity, obedience and silence: a bride of Christ. Silence. A life lived on my own, a lifetime of prayer and silence with only God as a companion along the way, and the only alcohol will be the brush of cheap red wine against my lips whenever I take Holy Communion. Nobody else: no family, no particular friendships with the other Sisters, just me and God. And all this for a woman who doesn't like her own company and whose belief in God and the power of prayer is not as steadfast and true as I gave Sister Mathilda to believe.

My mother thinks that having a daughter in Holy Orders will be like a fast-track to heaven when she dies. "See, God, what I have done? I have given you my daughter. I have raised a daughter so good and so holy she has become your bride— and now it's payback time." She has no idea about my sordid life in London, no idea.

Lying on the phone was easy. "Yes, mum, I've been to church this morning and the sermon was about selfishness. Yes, mum, I'm getting to bed early and taking care of myself. Yes, mum, I've made some friends in the parish and the priest is just like Father Dominic."

She liked that one: her favourite priest at home is Father Dominic. She always flutters around him when he turns up at coffee mornings and jumble sales, offering to fetch him a cup of tea or a chair and asking about his health. Visits home were more difficult. Extra layers of clothes to hide my thinness and my arms, all traces of make-up and nail varnish removed, and disappearing outside for a smoke whenever she went to the lavatory. I took my own bottles of vodka-laced coke to drink and told mum I'd gone off coffee and tea. Too much caffeine I said. I could only ever manage one night and then make some excuse for getting back to London. Back to no-hoper Carl.

I don't know what my dad thought. He used to go to Mass regularly but whether he went of his own free will as a believer or to keep up appearances I don't know. And it's too late to ask him now. Certainly his life would have been difficult if he hadn't gone: my mother was a force to be reckoned with. If she said it was time for church, it was time for church. We always had to be there early to get a pew right at the front so the priests could see us and take note of our piety. Poor old dad! We were too much alike—he'd have seen straight through my lies. Mum saw what she wanted to see.

Carl didn't see me at all. I think that to him I was a gullible fool, full of good intentions, and if he ever thought of me it was as a way of making his own life a little easier. We started off quite well, both of us in work, and living in a reasonable flat, but we spiralled down together through a series of dead end jobs to unemployment, and shifted from flat to bedsit to a squat. Whenever his drug-taking got out of control, I'd disappear for a few days, but then he'd come looking for me, promising to get himself clean. He never did. We ended up living on the streets, dirty and hungry and full of self-loathing. After he died I felt so guilty. I thought it was all my fault. If only I'd tried a bit harder, got him more help, looked after him better and got him to hospital sooner, he wouldn't have died. But by then I wasn't much use to anyone.

It took a couple of years after he died to get myself straight. I was never into drugs, I always thought that inside my head was weird enough already without drugs adding to the mixture— but alcohol was a pretty good substitute. The Salvation Army *was* my salvation. They picked me up off the streets, took me to a hostel, fed me, clothed me, cared for me. Me, Susan Ellis, not Carl's girlfriend or Mrs. Ellis's daughter. For the first time in many years I felt valued, a proper person. They accepted me as I was, imperfections and all. They also helped me return to the Catholic Church.

I was found a place on a week-long retreat in the Cotswolds. I was so happy and at peace there that I began to think maybe I could retreat from the world altogether. The more I thought about it, the better I liked the idea. My mental health was still a bit unsteady at the time and I was terribly worried about slipping back to my old habits of alcohol and self-harm. What could be better than a convent? Day would follow well-ordered day, year would follow year and I would find inner love and strength to overcome my black demons.

And so I lied. I set out quite deliberately to lie my way into a convent, and now my lies are catching up with me. St. Joseph's were so pleased at the thought of a new novitiate, reasonably young and from a good Catholic family, that they weren't very vigorous in questioning my vocation. After all those years of going to church with my mother I knew what sort of replies they needed to hear. I think the only time I was ever worried about being found out was during my medical examination. Sister Barbara was chaperoning me at the time. She's a bit short-sighted and didn't notice the doctor holding my forearms up to the light and running his finger across the scars. He was such a gentle man. After the examination was over and I was standing before him, he took both my hands firmly in his and smiled at me. Such a warm and friendly smile that I was taken aback for a moment. He said that if I needed any medical help to ask the Mother Superior to send for him. I think he might have thought that the blood samples he had just taken would show I was HIV positive, but I knew they wouldn't. I had only ever known Carl and he was on prescription drugs when I met him with access to clean needles. By the time things got really bad we weren't having sex anyway.

It is half past five. Sister Mathilda will be coming for me

soon. She warned me that these last few hours before such a big decision were bound to be full of doubts and worries. I don't think she realised that my worries were more about being found out for who I really am, rather than any worries about making my vows. Dear Sister Mathilda, she has spent such a lot of time with me over the last months and has been very patient with me. She has an uncanny way of looking at me over the top of her little horn-rimmed glasses, and I do sometimes feel that she might see glimpses of the real me. What am I going to tell her when she comes to collect me? That it was all a big sham, there was no vocation, thank you for the last couple of years, I am healthy now, my head is sorted out and I'm off home? But where is home? Where does my future lie? Here, where I have been respected and challenged by the strict discipline of women united in prayer? A bedsit up in London where I am a stranger amongst strangers? Or back with my mother?

It is six o'clock and I can hear a slow footfall along the corridor. I can feel my heart beating in my chest.

What am I going to do? What shall I say?

Summer Madness—July 1st 1916

David Richmond

After seven days of non-stop artillery fire, we'd got used to the noise and the tremors. Men scurried about like ants in the trenches, communicating by signs when they couldn't be heard above the boom of the guns. Fritz was taking a pounding, that was for sure, and I almost felt sorry for the poor bastards, thinking how it would've been if it had been us getting bombarded.

At 7 am it went quiet and we knew it was almost time to go. We checked our kit—bloody hell, there was a lot of it. I reckon each of us must have had 70 lbs of stuff to carry. They'd told us Haig wanted us to dig in and consolidate once we'd got across No Man's Land. We'd need all this stuff in case there was a problem setting up supply lines. All right for him and the officers on their bloody horses, with their batman to take care of their stuff. We'd have trouble getting out of the blooming trench!

The quiet was eerie after all that noise. There was something strange about hearing the familiar clink-clank of tin mugs knocking against rifles as men shuffled on their haunches, trying to ease the tension in muscles and minds. Next to me was crouched my pal, George Perks, and I could hear him whispering the "Our Father" to himself. I let him finish before I spoke: 'Don't worry, George. We'll be ok.'

George raised his chin to look at me. 'Remember what the Padre said last night, Wilf? About God bein' with us?'

'Course I remember, mate. Huns are wicked. Look what they did to Belgium. We can't let them do that to Blighty, can we?'

He clenched his teeth and nodded. 'No, I suppose not.'

I couldn't believe he sounded doubtful. 'What d'yer mean, mate, you s'pose not? What'd happen to our families if Fritz ever got 'is hands on 'em? It don't bear thinking about.'

'You're right, Wilf, I know. I think about that poster they put up outside the Town Hall at 'ome. You know the one: "The Hun and the Home". It said the Belgian women were murdered... and worse. I 'ate to think my Gladys might...well...you know.'

'That's the ticket, George! Huns are evil blighters and it's our duty to King and country to put an end to as many of 'em as we can.'

'Well, Wilf, not long now. Remember what the song says: "What's the use o' worryin'? It never was worthwhile."'

He grinned at me, flashing the gap in his teeth where a stray bit of shrapnel had almost ended his war months before. At the time we'd said he must be one lucky son of a gun, or his guardian angel was watching over him that day. One of the big shells we called a Jack Johnson had landed about fifty yards from our trench, and all kinds of muck came raining down on us. A piece of shrapnel passed clean through the rim of George's helmet and smashed out his two front teeth. They reckoned if it hadn't have hit the helmet first, he'd have been a goner. It would've taken half his face off. Lucky blighter, old George.

All of a sudden there was an almighty boom and the whole trench shook. Swarms of frantic rats appeared, squeaking and scuttling past as sandbags fell round us and the earth began to fall in. George's grin disappeared.

'Bloody 'ell, Wilf! What was that?'

Another earth-shaking explosion followed. The sides of the trench began to collapse and we had to scramble out from under the dirt.

'Reckon it must be those mines they've been putting under Fritz's lines, George. I heard they put tons of explosives in tunnels under their trenches.'

Several more huge explosions pounded our ears. George put his hands to the sides of his head. 'Poor sods! Must've been blown from 'ere to kingdom come.'

I fumbled inside my jacket and pulled out my old dad's pocket watch Mum had given me when I signed up. It was my lucky charm, that watch. Every bloke had something, some good luck piece. George had a bit of black bread he said his dad had brought back from the Boer War. Said it was what he'd had to eat when they were in Ladysmith under siege. Seemed to me to be a rum old thing to have as a charm, but there you go. It worked for him, he said. I looked at my watch: 7.30.

The bugles sounded the advance.

'That's us, George! Come on, me old mate. Let's go hunt the Hun.'

'What's left of him, don't yer mean? All that shelling ain't left us much to do, I reckon.'

With that, we fixed our bayonets and went over the top. We weren't running, just walking like, like you might do on a Sunday afternoon out for a stroll with your girl. We couldn't have run if we'd tried, not with all that clobber we were carrying.

Thick grey smoke was blowing across No Man's Land as we set out, so it was hard to see much. I could make out George, and the other blokes next to me and those just in front, but further than that you couldn't see what was happening. I couldn't see, but I could bloody well hear. I could hear machine guns, loads of them, it sounded like. Suddenly, all round me, blokes were screaming, calling out, and falling down. I looked at George and all his chest kind of suddenly exploded; his tunic burst open in a dozen places and blood and guts spurted out at me. He just looked kind of surprised—not in pain like you'd have thought—just surprised. He lifted his arms and stretched out his hands, as if he was going to pray or something, and then he just fell. That was it. I didn't stop and do anything— not that there was anything anyone could've done for him. He'd gone west for sure, and I had his innards plastered over my front, like a baby who's spilt his dinner down him.

Tommies were dropping all around me, chests blown open, heads blown off—horrible sights I pray to the Almighty I never have to see again as long as I live. It was hard to keep moving forward 'cos I kept stumbling over bodies. I fell and found myself at the bottom of a trench, with some other blokes, lying in a pool of blood and mud and body bits. We were all face-down in the slime, fingers clutching and scraping at the stuff as if trying to dig ourselves into the very earth itself. Some of the blokes were whimpering, some swearing, one or two praying. I couldn't help myself. I started to retch and then I was violently sick.

Something told me I'd got to get up though, and go on. There were still blokes moving forward. As fast as they got mown down, another wave came from behind to take their places, and then they all copped it. I couldn't understand it. The darts and farts had said the artillery barrage would knock out Fritz's positions and we'd just walk in. How bloody wrong could they be?

As I tried to run, I realised my right trouser leg was soaked with blood. I must've taken a hit without realising it. By now the smoke was so thick I couldn't see anything further than a few feet from me. To top it all, I'd lost all sense of direction and didn't know where I was heading. I just lumbered on, as best I could, until eventually I fell into another trench.

Imagine my feelings when, on looking up, I saw a German

officer facing me!

Frantically I grabbed my rifle and levelled the bayonet. I remembered my old sergeant's voice bellowing out his orders during training back home: 'Go for the throat or the chest, lads. That's where to stick the bastards!'

But I was too slow. The German was across the trench in a moment and delivered a swift and stinging punch to my jaw. He grabbed the rifle, threw it well out of reach along the trench, and reached into his tunic pocket. Stunned and exhausted, I leant back, resigned to the fact that he was going to shoot me.

Instead of pulling a pistol, though, he brought out his field dressing pack. He tore away my blood-soaked trouser and began tending to my injured leg. From a small metal bottle he poured iodine into the gaping wound, put a pad of gauze on, and carefully wrapped a bandage round it. All the time he spoke softly to me in German. I couldn't understand what he was saying, but his voice was soothing and calming, and I submitted to his ministerings as I might have done to those of my mother. When he was done, he offered me his water bottle and gently supported my head as I drank.

I looked at the face of the man I'd so recently tried to kill, and who was now tending me with as much compassion as I could have hoped for from medics on my own side. He was fairly young, not much older than me, I reckoned, with a neat little moustache, blond hair and very blue eyes. He smiled and, despite myself, I found myself smiling back at him.

'Thank you,' I managed, and then remembered one of the few words I had learned of his language. 'Danke.'

Again he smiled, spoke more of the soothing words I didn't understand, and I found myself wondering: Why had I wanted so desperately to kill this man? Why, because he wore a German uniform, had I been so ready to believe he was evil and would kill me? Clearly, he wasn't, and I realised that all we had been told about the Hun was just politicians' hot air. This war wasn't about defending our womenfolk and our young 'uns. We weren't blasting each other to bits in some god-forsaken part of France for them. I no longer knew what it was all about.

The hate I'd felt for the German hadn't been mine and I was cured of it now. In amongst all the horrors of that day he'd shown me compassion and reminded me that there's good and bad in all men. I'd learned there's more to being a man than fighting for your country, and sticking a bayonet into a stranger just because he's wearing a different uniform. It's about valuing life, caring for someone in need, looking after him and helping when you can, regardless of who he is. We can't damn everyone for the faults of a few.

Just a few hours before, George and I had set out to kill as many as we could. George's war had ended pretty quick when he copped it from the machine gunners. Now it seemed mine was over, as other Germans appeared in the trench and I was officially taken prisoner. Stretcher bearers lifted me up and carried me to a nearby field hospital where they patched me up and sent me further behind the lines to a holding camp for prisoners.

It was all over for me—the bombs, the bullets, the blood. I'd lost my best pal, and I'd lost my stomach for war. Amongst so much death, I'd learned that life is precious, and I now wanted life more than ever. I was lucky to have made it through that awful day - a day on which, I heard later, we lost sixty thousand men. Such waste! When they called an end to the madness on the Somme, in November, there'd been more than a million and a half casualties, and we'd gained no more than a few yards of land.

My Daughter was an Astronaut

Wilf Jones

My daughter was an astronaut:
She sailed the inky night;
Her smallest steps were giant leaps;
She put the dark to flight.

My daughter was the latest thing
To hit the silver screen;
She gave her heart to all the world,
The best there's ever been.

My daughter was a journalist
She braved the cease-fire line:
Endured the trials and found the words,
Revealed the cruel design.

My daughter was the midwife
Who saw the future born,
My daughter was a teacher;
She touched the brightest dawn.

My daughter had a concert grand
And played to charm the angels;
My daughter the couturier,

Her name the hottest label.

Morgan Grace was all of these,
Morgan Grace was none:
Her life is lived only in dreams;
My darling girl has gone.

My daughter was an astronaut,
She sailed the inky night.
She went ahead, ahead of me,
Her secret soul in flight

Across the darkest galaxy,
A place I've never been,
Who knows now what she has become,
Who knows what she has seen?

Something in the Woodshed.

Eleanor Castleden

Sidney had been looking forward to his retirement after a stressful life working in the City. His wife, Margaret had fallen in love with the Old Rectory with its huge garden in this Norfolk village, so they bought it and moved in.

Margaret chose the furnishings and décor, as usual, and she redesigned the garden. Sidney didn't really mind, he just wanted a peaceful life. It was spring and the sun was shining. All was quiet, except for the sound of birds singing, and the odd tractor in the distance.

One day he said, 'I've been thinking, dear. I've always wanted a real man's hobby, so I'm going to build something in the woodshed.

'What?' said Margaret.

'It's a surprise. It'll keep me busy and out of your hair. Every man needs his cave.'

'As long as you don't walk your muddy boots into the house, I don't mind what you do,' replied Margaret from behind her newspaper. She still wasn't used to having him around all day. She had already immersed herself in various local activities, like the Women's Institute and an art group.

'Right, that's decided then. I'll start work tomorrow; what's for tea, dear?'

Sidney's plans progressed well. He found the internet useful for some things much more interesting than spread sheets, and was getting excited about his project.

Margaret was glad he was happily occupied, but she was also curious, especially when a skip arrived and the woodshed was totally emptied. Then a local builder showed up and built on an extension, doubling its size. After that, Malcolm, a local carpenter came and spent several days sawing and hammering.

Sidney's pleasure and Margaret's curiosity grew in equal proportion but it was his surprise, she decided, so she would try to remain patient. In any case, she was far too busy learning about water colour painting, and making cakes and singing Jerusalem to be worrying about her husband and his shed.

However, when a van turned up with Bogan's Carpets painted on the side in bold red letters, she was more than a little suspicious. Why did Sidney need a new carpet? He couldn't be tinkering about with engines, or building a car then. She accosted him when he came in to wash his hands for lunch.

'I hope that shed will be finished soon,' she said. 'I'm getting fed up with all these men trampling through the orchard.'

'There won't be any more tradesmen after today,' said Sidney. 'But I've got to warn you, my shed will be a Mount Athos area: no women allowed.'

'I hope I shall be able to inspect it,' said Margaret.

'We'll see. I'm not sure if I mentioned it, I'm going to Norwich with Frank and George this afternoon. We need some boys' toys.'

'Boys' toys? Whatever next!' said Margaret.

The selection was enormous. George didn't know what to buy.

'I reckon you want a thingamabob with lots of zips and attachments,' said Frank.

'And something to hold it steady,' said George.

'Mini or full size, what do you reckon?' said Sidney.

'You know what they say, the bigger the better,' said Frank. 'Talking about size, do I need anything special for tits? They're my favourites.'

'A camera with zoom facility, and a wide-angled lens, I should think. That should take care of the detail and give us close-ups,' said George. 'And we could do with some camouflage gear, something with a hood and straps would be useful.'

They enjoyed trying out their new toys, and it was past bedtime before Sidney went in.

'Tomorrow's the day, Margaret," he said. "The boys are coming round after breakfast.'

'I'd better do my hair and put some lipstick on then,' said Margaret.

'They're not coming to see you.'

'Oh, Sidney, I know that. I was having a bit of a joke.'

A noisy old Land Rover drew up in the drive. Frank and George jumped out.

'Right dear, are you ready for your once only visit?'

'Can't wait,' said Margaret. She followed the three men through the orchard to the extended and improved woodshed.

'What's all this?' shrieked Margaret when she saw the plasma screen TV, the laptop, photographic equipment, tripods, microwave, a fridge full of beer, and the plush green carpet. 'What hobby needs all this stuff?'

'Birds,' said Sidney. 'This is a bird hide, Margaret. Aren't you pleased for me?'

'Depends what birds you're talking about," she said peering out through the opened shutters. "Strange how this shed, sorry bird hide, faces the Naturist club! I didn't know you could see it from our garden. Really, you men! You ought to know better at your age.'

'We're just wild about birds,' said Sidney with a grin. 'And it doesn't matter what species—wagtails, tits: the bigger the better. That's right, isn't it mates?'

Becoming a Doctor

Tony Irvin

I was seven when I informed my parents that I would be a doctor. When I raised the subject again years later, they had clearly forgotten.

'But you would have to go to university,' said my father.

'No one in our family has ever done that,' said my mother.

'We couldn't possibly afford the fees,' they both said.

I shrugged: 'I'll get a scholarship, then.'

Now, as I sat on the veranda watching the family cat trying to conceal itself behind a tree, I wondered if my brashness was about to be called to account and my childhood dream exposed for what it was—childish fantasy.

The tip of the cat's tail twitched as it eyed two hoopoes probing the lawn. It had done this for as long as I could remember: hoopoes, weavers, agama lizards, geckos, mice—it never caught anything.

I had been offered a place, had done the revision, had taken the exams—but had spurned my father's advice to "help" the examiners. Now, all I could do was wait, and wonder if the payment of a few thousand shillings might not have been a sensible investment towards achieving my life's ambition.

The cat made a half-hearted rush at the hoopoes. They flew up and settled on another part of the lawn. The cat sat down and licked a paw. I smiled at its feigned indifference, then waved to Joseph the gardener, who, dressed in shorts and Wellington boots, was trundling backwards and forwards pushing a hand-mower (one of those with a long handle and a cross-piece that you never see these days). Joseph stopped to wave and grin. Then, with the sweat pouring off his body, resumed the task that never seemed to daunt or tire him.

The garden was mainly lawn; it started at the front of the house, spread round the sides and flowed down to the lake where it merged with papyrus, an impenetrable wall of green, broken only by the tunnels through which hippos emerged at night. I liked to imagine them frolicking on the lawn in the moonlight, but probably they just snuffled around for any grass that had escaped Joseph's attention.

I heard my mother calling from inside the house.

'Sunil, it's come! It's here!' She came bustling onto the veranda, clutching baby Rajev under one arm and waving a letter in her free hand. The rest of the family (except my father, who was at the sugar factory) hurried after her. Close behind, came Ezekiel, drying his hands on his apron.

I took the letter.

Everyone lined up to watch.

'See the stamp!' cried my mother.

It had to be the letter. No one else would have written to me from Kenya.

'Open it, Sunil!' urged my sister.

'Go on,' chorused the rest of the family. 'Open it.'

Ezekiel nodded encouragement. Joseph stopped mowing.

Years later I still remember those details. I even remember that an ibis flew down onto the lawn to peer at the mower.

What if I'd failed? How could I face the family, who, once they had accepted my ambition, had put such hope and expectation into my achieving success?

With clumsy fingers and a sinking feeling in my stomach,

I opened the envelope and extracted a single sheet of paper.

Too little writing. I should have followed my father's advice.

I closed my eyes.

'I've passed,' I whispered.

It seemed ages before I could get to sleep that night. I lay on my bed thinking and gazing at the moon through the haze of the mosquito net. I'm going to medical school; I'm going to be a doctor; I'm going to bring honour to my family. I closed my eyes: I'm going to be a doctor; I'm going to be a doctor. The litany eventually lulled me to sleep. But no sooner had I drifted off, than a persistent banging broke through my subconscious. My first thought was that it was a hippo. Occasionally, one would try to break into the garage—we'd no idea why.

As I lay in the darkness listening, a doubt began to creep into my mind. These were anxious times. I pulled the pillow over my head, trying to shut out the noise, and attempted to get back to sleep. The doubt could wait until morning.

But it couldn't.

'Sunil, Sunil!'

I sat up, trying to orientate.

Someone was outside.

'Sunil, wake up!'

I pushed the net aside, scrambled out of bed and peered through the window.

My uncle's car was on the driveway, and he was hammering at the front door.

'What is it?' I called.

'You must be leaving, the soldiers are coming.' The muffled voice was urgent and fearful.

I could see my aunt in the car. The light from the porch made tears on her cheeks glisten.

I rushed through to my parents' room – they were already awake.

'The soldiers are coming!'

'Oh, my God!' cried my father, struggling with his dressing gown. My mother was frantic. 'Oh no!' she whimpered. 'Please no!' She rushed to wake up the other children. My father began dragging out suitcases from the hall cupboard.

I ran and unlocked the door and my uncle burst into the house. 'There is no time for packing,' he cried. 'Just come!'

'But we must be taking some clothes,' cried my father.

'No, see—already they are at Joginder's house.' My uncle pointed, and we saw flames erupt from the thatch on the roof of a house no more than a quarter of a mile away.

'You must be coming!' urged my uncle. 'Leave everything. Just come.'

My father rushed outside.

By now, the whole house was awake, and the twins were screaming.

Ezekiel and his wife had hurried round from the servants' quarters to see the cause of the commotion.

'Ezekiel, please help with the children. We have to leave,' cried my mother, her face also streaked with tears. I remember that I was the only one not crying—perhaps I had been too frightened.

As I went to help my mother, I heard the sound of a car, the roar of an engine, the crunch of gears, the hiss of tyres spinning on gravel.

Too late! They're already here!

But it was our own car that tore round the side of the house, my father at the wheel. He had never abused his elderly and beloved Morris like this before. He skidded to a halt and leapt out. His dressing gown snagged and tore on the door catch. 'Hurry, hurry!' he cried, bundling my mother and Rajev into the back.

'Please no, please no!' My mother still whimpered as she took the screaming twins from Ezekiel. Ashok and my sister

Sunita scrambled into the front—she was holding the toy rabbit she slept with. I squeezed in beside them. 'We will be back, Ezekiel,' cried my father. 'Look after yourselves!' He leapt back into the front seat and slammed the door, leaving one of his slippers on the drive.

'Yes, bwana,' said the bewildered Ezekiel, as the gears crunched and we sped off after my uncle's car which was already out of sight.

I glanced back at the elderly couple standing in the driveway looking fearful, their faces faintly lit by the glow of flames. Ezekiel went and picked up the slipper. They had been with the family since my father was a child.

The car turned onto the road and they disappeared from view.

Twenty minutes later, those two gentle people, whose only transgression was forty years devoted service to an Asian family, were hacked to death with machetes (pangas, we called them) by Idi Amin's thugs. Two hours later, the beautiful house at Jinja, overlooking the source of the Nile, was no more than a smouldering ruin. I thank God that it was some years before I learned of these terrible events.

We drove all that night and reached the border just as it was getting light. I never understood why we were waved through but my uncle and aunt were stopped. My father waited for over four hours, then had to drive on. I never saw my uncle and aunt again, and never knew what happened to them.

And so, with only the clothes I was wearing and a place at Nairobi medical school, I came to Kenya. Our nationality had been taken away, and my father's briefcase of Ugandan shillings did little more than buy us a few clothes. But it was there, thanks to the kindness of my mother's cousin who welcomed us into her family in Parklands on the outskirts of Nairobi, that I completed my medical training and fulfilled my childhood dream.

Mud

George Wicker

In plain sight of officers, for memory
of all Englishmen who fought in wars
the soldiers abandoned their posts. Fearing only
that cowardice and trench fever
stood between themselves and death,
they ran. God how they ran,
as the officers knelt behind them
and raised their arms, jealous perhaps that
rank and upbringing prevented the same
coarse dishonour flowing
through their veins.
                            For a moment
they held each deserter in the sights
of polished and well-maintained pistols,
knuckles hinged on triggers, breath held
long and slow in anticipation
of their targets.

None fired, but rose instead as one,
took off their caps, tunics, badges and
threw down each gun, some in disgust
with themselves and their learning
took off belts and trousers, went naked,

wallowed in mud at the bottom of trenches
while the soldiers fled, unharmed.

Dilemma

Pat Christie

It was a Thursday morning when the box arrived and her world changed for ever.

That's a good first line for a story. Shouldn't be a problem. As I drive away from the writing group, various scenarios go through my mind. The next morning I switch on the computer, straight after breakfast. Might as well get on with it while I'm enthusiastic.

It was a Thursday morning when the box arrived and her world changed for ever. Mary opened it and looked sadly at the plastic urn containing her husband's ashes. Was it only ten days since he had died? Until now she had been numb. Too much to do and think about. Arrangements to be made. People to contact. Letters to write. But now with the arrival of the ashes, the full import of her changed life began to dawn on her...

This is naff. I'll get myself a coffee and start again. The phone rings. I hang out the washing. A neighbour drops by for a chat. You know how it goes. But I was back at the computer after lunch.

It was Thursday morning etc. Old Mrs Evans shook the parcel and wondered who on earth had sent it. She hadn't ordered anything. It wasn't near her birthday. And, anyway, she wasn't in the habit of receiving letters, never mind parcels. It rattled a bit and was quite heavy, so she set it carefully on the table and fetched some scissors.

Never one to waste anything Mrs Evans cut the brown paper and folded it. She studied the blue box in front of her and...

And what? Don't like this one either. I look at the screen for ages and try to remember some of the ideas I had had last night. How about this one?

Thursday morning etc. Jan answered the door and signed the note for the registered parcel. 'Have a good day,' the postman said as he went on his way.

'And you.' she called after him. Humming to herself, she went into the kitchen and put on the kettle. She ripped off the paper and opened the tiny box inside.

'Oh, my God!' There, lying on a bed of cotton wool, was a tiny silver heart-shaped locket. The very locket she had left with her baby daughter when she handed her over for adoption all those years ago...

Hmm! Not sure about this one. I'll call it a day for just now and hope that I find inspiration soon. Plenty of time before the writing group meets again.

It's amazing how time does fly, though. Here I am with only one day to go and the pressure is on. All those great scenarios I had worked out on the way home have been lost in the dim mists of my memory. I'll check the list to see what makes a good story—"hook, drama, motivation, action, resolution, sympathetic characters". Right, here we go.

It was a Thursday morning when the box arrived and her world changed for ever.

She couldn't believe what she was seeing when she opened the back door. He must have left it there during the night and the thought made her shiver with fear.

How had he known where she lived? After that night when she had fled from him in terror she had managed to make a new life for herself but now...

But now? Blanksville again. I sharpen a few pencils, throw

out some old papers, tidy my writing desk and discover a sheet of Mills and Boon guidelines amongst the clutter—"Warm tender emotions, no sexual explicitness, heart-warming stories to be written with freshness and sincerity". Sounds rather boring but I'll have a bash at some 'romantic suspense'.

Thursday morning etc. Sharon's heart throbbed passionately as she opened it. The red velvet box contained a sparkling diamond ring. A small card fell to the floor. With trembling fingers she picked it up: "To my one and only true love. Be mine for all eternity. Your devoted and adoring J." Sharon's eyes misted with tears as she slipped the ring on her finger and held it close to her heart…

What a load of crap! I can't write romantic stuff. It's just not me. Back to the blood and guts of real life.

It was Thursday morning etc. When the knock came at the door, Jane jumped up.

'I'll get it,' said the WPC who had been her constant companion for three days, ever since her daughter had gone missing. Sergeant Grant came back into the room, clutching a small parcel. She put on some gloves and opened it carefully.

'Hmm, postmarked London,' she muttered, 'I'll get forensics onto this.' Inside was a box with a note attached:

'We have got your daughter and here is the proof. Next time it could be a finger or an ear. Wait for instructions and DO NOT contact the police.'

Jane collapsed on to the sofa with a shriek as the WPC showed her a lock of Lynn's distinctive red hair. She looked questioningly at her and Jane nodded wordlessly. Tears streamed down her face …

Bloody hell, this is hopeless and, anyway, I've run out of time—and ideas. Tuesday evening has arrived, so guess I'll just have to take along a couple of poems "wot I wrote" a few weeks ago. Did I say this would be no problem?

Contributors

Julian Corbell spent all his adult working life in State Secondary Schools, teaching French and Psychology. A little while ago he retired at the age of 62. He tries to follow Wordsworth's ideal of "recollecting emotion in tranquillity" by turning the more memorable episodes of his life into short stories. Writing initially to inform his three children about his early years, he is now completing his third volume, having self-published the second under the title of "Unreliable Memoir".

Eleanor Castleden: I have been a member of Write Now! for over six years and enjoy the motivation and camaraderie of a writers' group such as ours. My writing has covered many genres over the years, including poetry, short stories and travelogues. I am very pleased and proud to be part of our first Anthology, and hope that our readers will find this interesting, inspirational and entertaining.

David Richmond: I was born in Surrey but moved to Suffolk almost forty years ago. Since retirement I have been able to devote more time to writing, which has been a love of mine since I was a teenager, and have enjoyed some small successes in on-line competitions.

Laura Haines is an artist/illustrator who recently moved from Winchester, Hampshire to Stowmarket, Suffolk. She graduated from Kingston University in 2009 and recently completed an MA in archaeological illustration at Oxford Brookes University. Laura is currently working at the Museum of East Anglian Life as a curatorial assistant. She enjoys writing poetry and stories, and illustrating them!

Carolyn Belcher, retired drama teacher and theatre practitioner. Married, three children and three grandchildren. Has had stories and poems published in literary magazines and a monologue performed at a New Writing Festival, in Reading.

A retired English teacher, **Barry Baddock** now messes around, seeking legal ways to fill the time. One of them has been to publish a comic novel ('Nomads' Rest': Troubador Publishing, 2011) which is largely set in Suffolk, the county of his birth.

Nigel George, Bouncy, fat and frequently rude, Also a writer, lawyer, cook, rambler, lover of good beer, fine wine, exotic places and the absurd.

Tony Irvin is a vet who went to East Africa for two years and stayed for twenty where he became an expert on a disease of cattle that no one outside Africa has ever heard of. He has camped among elephants, canoed among hippos, eaten crocodile, and photographed a rhino in his pyjamas. He writes adventure stories set in Africa; The Ant-Lion and The Elephant Shrew, the first two books in the African Safari Adventure series for 8-12 year-olds, are available from Waterstones or on-line from Matador.

Wilf Jones is an obscure fantasy writer and poet from Leigh in Lancashire, currently living in familial harmony in the more placid climes of West Suffolk. Having spent most of his life selling books for other people, he has recently determined to spend more time on his own work. His greatest efforts are directed towards the continued development of the epic fantasy *A Song of Ages*.

Jo Marsh graduated from Cambridge University in 2011 and is currently a Teacher of English at a secondary school in Norfolk. She started her writing career under the mentorship of Sally Cline, author of the acclaimed book The Arvon Book of Life Writing co-written with Carole Angier. Following broadcast of 'Life for a Life' on the radio during 2010 this story has now been adapted for written publication. She is currently working on a novel with a contemporary 'jigsaw effect' twist.

George Wicker is a published poet, and author of an unpublished fantasy novel *Inside Out*. Co-founder of Write Now!, he works in the print industry and has too many hobbies. In the 1980s he edited, typeset and printed *Inverse*, an occasional arts magazine. He has also printed and self-published *Jade*, a collection of poems inspired by Chinese thought and culture, and a further volume of poems, *Signs*.

Russell Kemp was born and bred in Suffolk in 1949 and is a founder member of 'Write Now!' Currently employed as a programmer of CNC engineering machinery, he makes better use of his spare time writing preferably humorous short stories, some of which have been published for financial gain. He enjoys the talented diversity of the group.

Pat Christie is a long standing member of Write Now! She has produced hugely entertaining plays and verse pieces for local performance, and has kept the group in stitches through many a long winter evening.

Lisa Climie began her working life as a backing vocalist to the beehive Queen of Neasden, Mari Wilson. She soon moved into a career in acting appearing in several productions at the Edinburgh Fringe and on TV in *The Bill*, *Bergerac* and in the lead role of an award winning BBC short film. Later moving to a career in counselling, she specialised in working with those with addiction problems. She co-founded, and is now on the board of trustees, of Suffolk based Focus12, a centre for the treatment of addiction. Coming from a family of writers: father David, a comedy script writer; brother Simon a song writer and sister Sarah a journalist, the time has come for Lisa to join the family trade. She lives in Suffolk with Son Seth, another budding writer, and dog Nelson.

Rose O'Meara has lived in Suffolk for many years. She loves reading, writing, gardening and mugs of strong tea. She is trying, without notable success, to be able to do all four things at once.

Copyright